BLANC LABELLE

AND THE TROLL'S DAUGHTER

by Nicholas Westbrook

<u>Chapter 1</u>

"Can you come clean up aisle 16?"

"What?" Matt asked. He was only three hours into his shift stocking the shelves and it already felt like eight. With all the restaurants closed down again, the pandemic had increased store traffic to the point that keeping the shelves from going bare felt like a full-time job without Matt's other duties. Still, most people ignored him and he preferred that to listening to someone's latest conspiracy theory in response to the store's mask policy. The only reason Matt took these shifts was so he wouldn't need to talk with customers like this girl.

"There's a mess in aisle 16," the girl urged. Her long, blonde hair was tied up into a messy bun to keep the strands out of her emerald green eyes. She looked about sixteen, but if they went to the same school, Matt didn't recognize her from any of his classes. She was wearing a bright yellow raincoat, a floral t-shirt, jeans, and water-logged sneakers. Matt wasn't sure if he'd heard her correctly or not with the thick, cloth mask hiding her mouth.

Matt sighed and ran a hand over his curly, dark hair. He was wearing jeans and a white t-shirt under his wrinkled, dark green work apron. He had always been a skinny kid with a round face and dark brown eyes. When he spoke in the store, it was with the practiced grace of someone who'd been working in retail for too long. "Yeah," Matt sighed, "we don't have an aisle 16."

"I think you should check again," the girl said, a little firmer. "Let me show you."

"I have to—"

"Please," she pleaded. "You need to see this."

Something about the urgency in her voice surprised Matt and he decided to follow her rather than endlessly stack the cans to his right. He tugged his cotton mask a little further up his nose and walked a few steps behind her. Why she'd chosen him to handle the current problem made no sense. Even if the store had an aisle 16, Matt was sure that someone else was closer that could handle it just as well. Still, he followed the girl to the mysterious aisle when his curiosity eclipsed his irritation.

Once bottles of soda and bags of chips flanked them on either side of aisle 15, the girl finally stopped walking. Checking both ends of the aisle, she held a finger over her mask to shush him. Her eyebrows raised to ask for Matt to be quiet and he nodded to accept her request.

"I know there's no aisle 16," she whispered.

"Oh good, you can read numbers," Matt rolled his eyes.

"But I do need your help."

The girl pulled off her mask. Her eyes were normal enough, but the lower half of her face startled Matt. Her nose was flat and broad like the gorilla Matt had seen at the zoo when he was eleven. Her mouth was punctuated by two sharp teeth protruding up from her lower jaw. Each tusk was as long and thick as the last knuckle of Matt's pinky.

"Please don't panic!" The strange girl urged, pulling her mask back over her face. Matt could still see the outline of her tusks, but anyone who didn't know wouldn't give her masked face a second look. "If you do, they'll find me for sure."

"I—you—you're—"

"Half," the girl said, looking over her shoulder. "Half-troll, I mean. On my mother's side. Be glad I only inherited her teeth and not her temper. I need your help."

"What are you? What do you mean troll?"

"Look," she urged, "What's important is that I'm not going to hurt you. My name is Mira."

"Mira," Matt exhaled. "Okay, so why are you here? Shouldn't you be under a bridge or something?"

"That's offensive stereotyping!" Mira snapped. She relaxed her clenched fist and Matt could hear her slowly exhale through her mask. "Look, everyone is wearing a mask these days, so I figured it would be a perfect time to come above ground for something important. Vampires and elves come up all the time, but this has been my first chance to ever go up to the Above."

"There are vampires and elves? I've never seen one."

"Maybe you just never knew? Some folk have all the luck."

"Why do you need me?"

"I need help getting across town. There's someone very important I need to find."

"Can't I just…give you bus fare and forget you were here?"

"I'm afraid that won't work."

"I don't know, I'm very good at forgetting things."

"They're looking for people like me on buses. Please, I need your help." Mira paused and read his name tag. "I'm begging you, Matt. I need help."

"Who's looking for you?"

"Go take a peek at the main doors. There are two men in black windbreakers by the exit. They're not shopping, just looking around."

Matt walked down to the end of the aisle. At both of the automatic doors, there was a man stationed in a black windbreaker and a disposable white mask. One was wearing dark sunglasses, but Matt could see the other man's eyes scanning people's faces as they walked out the door. The man without glasses turned towards him and Matt frantically ducked behind the aisle display. After he checked again to ensure the men weren't charging to get him, Matt rushed back to Mira.

"Those guys are after you? Why?"

"Because I'm half-troll. Their whole organization hunts and kills people like me. Please, Matt, I need help. If I'm caught, they'll kill me and dissect me. Maybe not in that order either."

"Okay, what do you want me to do?"

"Do you have a car?" Mira asked. "Can you take me out of here and drive me across town?"

"What about my boss?"

"Say you're feeling sick. They'd have to send you home, right?"

"Yeah, but I could get fired if I'm caught ditching."

"Look, do this for me and you can have all my money."

"Trolls have money?"

"Half-troll," Mira corrected, glaring, "and, yeah. I have a little saved up. The guy I'm looking for might offer you more. I know it's a big request, but I'm out of options that don't involve me getting experimented on."

Matt looked over his shoulder again, paranoid. Mira was in real danger, he could see that. There were risks: losing his job, getting mixed up in something sinister, getting himself hurt. He thought for a moment about what to do. Matt knew she didn't have any other options. In the end, he chose to help Mira because she had asked him for it. "Okay," Matt whispered. "Follow me."

Weaving his way through the aisles, Matt brought Mira over to the produce section and checked around to make sure they had a clear path to the double doors that led to the stock room. They moved together into the employees-only section of the store. Matt walked through the towers of boxes left for him to unpack and shelve for his shift. While he needed the money, the sight of the boxes made Mira's strange offer more compelling.

"Wait here," Matt said, hiding Mira between two pallets of plastic-wrapped cereal boxes. "I could get in trouble for ditching my shift, but we'll both get in trouble if you're caught. Wait here while I talk to my boss."

Taking a deep breath, Matt thought about the best approach to get out of his shift. He walked into his manager's office, knocking on the door frame to get Jake's attention. Jake had a bit of a potbelly and most of his sandy blond hair was swept up in his desperate combover. He usually wore a white shirt and tie but had recently accented his attire with a face mask made by his youngest daughter.

"Hey Jake, I'm not feeling too hot. I'm thinking I should get out of here before it gets worse."

"Are you sure you can't just tough it out?" Jake asked, exasperated. "I've got people jumping ship left and right. I'm struggling to keep the store running."

"I'd feel better if I got tested."

Jake's mask puffed out a little when he sighed heavily, shaking his head. "Sorry, but I need bodies in the store and working."

"I just wanna get tested. I wouldn't want anyone to get sick. I can't imagine what would happen if corporate found out we gave a customer Covid."

Jake sighed again. "God, I'm gonna be happy when all this is over. Fine, get checked. Unless you can get me a doctor's note, I'm gonna need you tomorrow."

"I swear, I'll be back the moment a doctor gives me the all-clear. It might be stress, but I want to be safe."

"We're all stressed," Jake grumbled, sternly, "but I can't have you getting anyone sick. Go get a test. If you're not back by tomorrow, I'll hire someone else to replace you, got it?"

"Yes, sir."

Jake mumbled something else, but Matt couldn't hear it. Jake may have been a hard ass as a manager, but he was responsible to a fault. Matt felt bad exploiting him, but he had a feeling that Mira's request mattered more than the grocery store's bottom line. He was still risking his job to help a stranger, though Matt doubted he would want to go back to his job after the discovery of troll girls and secret organizations.

"All clear, come on," Matt waved to Mira. She staggered out of her hiding space, adjusting her mask to properly cover her snout. Walking out by way of the loading dock, Matt checked ahead for the men in windbreakers or anything else out of the ordinary. When he saw the path to his car was safe, he led Mira out while making sure to avoid the security camera. He opened his door quickly and ducked into his car with a breath of relief.

"Do you have an address for this friend of yours?" Matt asked, fumbling with his keys as Mira buckled her seatbelt.

"We have to go to the west side of the Valiant Apartment Complex," Mira said, watching out their windows. "The only other directions I got were 'follow the sword.'"

"Follow the sword?" Matt said. "Weirdly prophetic. You couldn't take a bus all the way downtown?"

"The buses aren't safe, I told you. I was riding one when those guys from the grocery store hopped on. I don't think it's a coincidence that they got off at the same stop."

"Why are they after you?"

"The Oak Hand hates anything that's not human. If they don't kill us on sight, they study us to learn how to kill us better. It's been that way for hundreds of years. I thought they'd be less active with the virus, but it looks like even a pandemic won't stop them from hunting Underfolk."

"Underfolk?" Matt asked, starting his car.

"Sure," Mira shrugged as if it were the most natural phrase. "Trolls and other Underfolk live in the Under, humans live in the Above."

"There's more Underfolk than just trolls?"

"It would take too long to list everyone in the Under and I'd forget something."

"I feel like I need a guidebook to get through today," Matt said, putting his car into reverse. He backed out of his parking space and started weaving his way through the crowded lot. As he started driving towards the main entrance, Mira's hand snapped out and grabbed his shoulder.

"What?" Matt asked, still moving forward.

"That's not a cop."

Matt hadn't seen it at first, but he followed Mira's shaky finger to the cop car parked at the exit. He was stopping cars every so often, congesting the parking lot more than usual. The man was wearing a tan trooper's uniform with a broad hat. He'd lean over, peer in each car, then wave people through. He'd parked his car on the grass lawn, an ugly beige sedan that looked more suited for the junkyard.

"I don't know how much you Underfolk see of the Above," Matt assured her, "but that's how cops dress these days. The car is just unmarked."

"Except that there aren't any antennas on the trunk," Mira said. "Even unmarked cars need some kind of antenna array to communicate with other officers. Plus, he has bumper stickers on the front which is a violation of code. I live underground, not under a rock."

"That's the only way out of the store. What do you want me to do?"

"Drive through! Ram his car and drive away as fast as you can!"

"That's not really how we do things up here," Matt said. "He's just talking to people."

"Oak Hand don't just *talk* when they see people like me."

"Let me try it my way?" Matt pleaded. "If I can't talk our way out of it? Then we'll turn into Bonnie and Clyde."

"More like Thelma and Louise."

"I promise, I'm gonna see you through to the end of this, but we need to avoid drawing attention to ourselves. Just focus forward and keep your mask up."

Mira started to protest, but Matt slowed his car for the potential patrolman. She set her hands on her lap, twisting her fingers together. Matt rolled his window down and looked up at the impersonator.

"Afternoon," the officer said, setting a hand on the roof of the car and leaning down. He was wearing a face mask and sunglasses, but Matt could still see his eyes peering around the car.

"Afternoon," Matt said, keeping calm. "Is there a problem?"

"No, we're just making sure everyone is following distancing behaviors. Where are you two off to?"

"She's uh…she's not feeling great," Matt said. "The boss worries she might have caught something, so he's sending her home and I'm her only option for a ride."

"What symptoms?"

"Trouble breathing," Matt said, listing the virus symptoms, "dizziness, nausea. We're all wearing masks and gloves on staff, but a handful of shoppers refuse to follow the rules."

"Yeah, I've been seeing a lot of that," the officer said. "She does look a little pale."

"I'm taking her home now so she can rest."

"Where does she work?"

"Bakery," Mira stammered out. "I was near someone without a mask on the bus this morning."

"Well, I hope you feel better," the officer said, considering the situation. "Best get on home. Be sure to keep the windows down. No sense in both of you getting sick."

Matt nodded his thanks and drove forward. Mira let out a shaking breath and rubbed her arms. "That was so scary."

"Sorry, it was the only way out," Matt said, pulling over as soon as the grocery store was out of sight. "What made you say bakery?"

"I like muffins," Mira shrugged. "I think if I could live in the Above, I'd be a baker. Do what makes you happy, right?"

Matt grinned and took out his phone. He punched in a number and put his phone on speaker. The line rang twice before the person on the other end picked up.

"Hedgefield Police Department," a woman answered.

"Hi, my name is Matt Brand. There's an unmarked police car with an officer stopping people at the Hedgefield Grocer. I'm curious if it's legitimate or not."

"Did he threaten you? Are you in trouble?"

"No, but he didn't seem like a real cop."

"What was his license plate?"

"6DLG990. It was a New York plate," Matt said, checking over his shoulder to make sure they weren't being pursued as he heard the woman typing on the other end of the call. He gave Mira a reassuring nod as he waited.

"Nothing is coming up in our records," the operator concluded. "I'll send someone over to check it out. Even if he's not threatening people, impersonating an officer is a very serious offense. Thanks for making the call, Mr. Brand."

"Thank you," Matt said. He hung up the phone and looked over at Mira. "That should scare them off. If they're smart, they'll try their luck somewhere else or lay low for a few hours. Should buy us some time."

"Thanks," Mira smiled, broadly. "You didn't have to do that, so… thanks."

Even with her mask on, Matt could tell that Mira was smiling so big that there were little creases around her eyes. He liked it when she smiled. "So," Matt cleared his throat. "Downtown express, next stop: Valiant Apartment Complex."

Chapter 2

"Mira? We're here."

Mira perked up, climbed out of the car, and looked around, wide-eyed. All around her were towers of glass and steel so bright that sunlight turned the city into a giant reflector ball. There were few plants, only a few carefully monitored trees, and shrubberies in clay pots outside of a big office building. Following the ascent of the tower, Mira thought she would fall over backward, looking up the length of the skyscraper as it disappeared into the endless blue sky.

"It's so big!"

"Yeah," Matt confirmed. "The Bryant Building is the tallest in the city: thirty stories. My class went up to the top observation deck for a field trip once and—"

"No," Mira shook her head. "The sky! I've never seen anything like it."

Mira knew the sky existed, but she wasn't prepared for the scope of it. Now that she felt a little safer, she could take in just how big the sky was. It looked like a massive curve of blue cloth thrown over the city, engulfing everything beneath it. Birds helped give it a sense of scale, but then she would see a tiny speck of a plane and the sky turned limitless again.

"I guess it is," Matt chuckled, following the half-troll girl's gaze to the cloudless sky. "I know you've never been to the city before, but have you really never been above ground?"

"Not until today, no," Mira mumbled, a little sheepish. "Most of my time in the Above has been looking over my shoulder for Oak Hand."

"Maybe when this is all sorted out, I'll take you to the ocean," Matt said. "If you think the sky is big here, you should see it when you're not surrounded by buildings."

"I've never seen the ocean," Mira said, excited. She settled and focused on her mission. "But we should find LaBelle first. I can play tourist once we figure everything out."

"Right," Matt said. "So we're looking for a sword?"

"That's the most direction I have," Mira said. She pointed to the apartment complex covered with graffiti across the street from where Matt parked. "And that's the Valiant Apartment Complex."

"Well," Matt shrugged. "Unless you brought your own? I don't see any swords. They haven't been used in about five hundred years. Unless it's a novelty sword from the pier carnival?"

"There!" Mira pointed at the Valiant Apartment Complex. Across the side of the building, someone had painted a stylized warrior, perched in a fighting position. His shield was covering his body, but his sword was outstretched and pointing down the street, wrapping around the exposed brick corner. Mira rushed off, but Matt grabbed her shoulder and pulled her back onto the sidewalk as a car blared its horn at her.

"Sorry!" Matt shouted. The driver waved his hand and yelled before continuing down into the city's downtown. Mira looked sheepishly at Matt as he pressed the big, red button for the crosswalk signal.

"I got excited, sorry," Mira said. "I owe you twice now."

"Let's not keep score," Matt said as they crossed the street.

Mira looked up at the graffiti, following the illustration of the sword around the edge of the building. There was another warrior drawn in a similar style, locked in combat with the other figure, but the point of the spear was pointed away from the conflict. The tip of the weapon touched one of the windows of the smaller office building next door. Mira looked at Matt and smiled.

"Not very subtle," Matt said, looking at the giant arrow pointing at the window.

"Only if you're looking for it," Mira explained and rushed towards the building's door. The entrance wasn't locked and Mira only waited long enough for Matt to follow her into the stairwell. They rushed up the stairs together, Mira's sneakers squeaking all the way upstairs and Matt close on her heels. When she reached the third floor, Mira turned and rushed down the hall. The hallway was an olive green color with frosted half-globe lamps between each of the doors and a beige tiled floor. Benches dotted the hallway, simple slats of wood for people to wait outside of too cramped offices. She skidded to a halt at the last office on the top floor, where the spear's tip would be pointing.

"Detective Blanc LaBelle," Mira read aloud from the plaque next to the door. "No knocking or unsolicited entry. Sit and you will be served soon."

"What do they mean by soon?" Matt asked.

Mira shrugged and walked to a bench on the wall, sitting with her hands in her lap.

"Are you just gonna sit and wait?"

"Do I have a choice?" Mira asked.

Matt looked back down the hall and sat next to Mira. "Then I guess we'll wait and see."

"You don't have to stay," Mira said. "I need to talk to LaBelle, but you don't have to be here."

"Hey, I promised I would make sure I get you to this guy. So, I guess we're stuck together until this LaBelle person shows up."

"Thanks," Mira said, bumping his leg with her knee. "For everything."

"I'd be lying if I said I wasn't curious about where this was going. Trolls, vampires, elves, some secret organization, and now a magic detective? This is getting way more interesting than a grocery store. So, who's LaBelle?"

"Blanc LaBelle is supposed to be someone who fixes problems."

"So he kills people?"

"No, like, if you have a problem in the Under or the Above. Blanc LaBelle is someone who can fix things between the two. Things like if you're not where you're supposed to be in the Above or a human sees you by mistake or…or if you're looking for someone."

"Kind of like a private eye?"

"Yeah, sort of. He helps Underfolk, but he's also talked about like he's the boogieman. Only a handful of people I know have seen his face, but almost everyone knows his name. I heard it whispered by trolls and pixies alike, so I figured he would be the person to help me. Most folks in the Above aren't supposed to know about Underfolk, so when we can't ask the human police for help, LaBelle talks to them for us."

"Does he explain things to non-cops, too? Cause I could use a primer course on whatever is going on here."

Mira laughed and tugged her mask up a little. Matt let out a breath and leaned back against the bench. "It'd be nice to know if someone was in there. I hope we don't have to wait out here all day."

"Do you have an appointment?" A voice said from over Mira's head.

Mira whipped her head around quickly. Matt looked just as confused and peered up over her shoulder. The dome light over their bench flickered a little and something buzzed like a large fly was trapped in the glass. The glow shifted around and rose out of the opening of the light fixture. The ball of light descended quickly to Mira's knee and dimmed. A woman, small enough to stand on Mira's hand, with wings like a purple dragonfly. She flattened out her lilac dress as she landed on Mira's leg and fluffed her dark hair in a wave.

"I—no," Mira said. "I'm sorry, we didn't know we needed one."

"Not a problem," the fairy said, sweetly. Her purple cheeks almost looked rosy as she gazed up at Mira with eyes like little pinpricks of white light. "We mostly get walk-ins these days. What is the nature of your emergency?"

"I'm being chased by the Oak Hand," Mira explained. "I need Detective LaBelle to help me find safety."

"Ah, poor thing," the fairy shook her head, sadly. "Those ruthless thugs just enjoy walking all over us to prove they're so superior. It's a shame you're involved in their petty squabble. Let me see if he's available."

The small woman started to glow again, fluttered her wings, and hovered away from Mira. The fairy moved to the opposite side of the hallway, wound up, and propelled herself forward. There was a light click as she passed through the mail slot and the fairy's glow disappeared behind the detective's door.

"I didn't think any fairies lived in the Above, except for a few spies," Mira said, looking excitedly at Matt. "At least we know one thing."

"Yeah," Matt chuckled uneasily, "we know we're in the right place."

###

Every immortal has a weakness. Vampires had a notoriously long list: from garlic and holy water to wooden stakes and decapitation. Even if elves were spared from the ravages of time and disease, a skilled enough opponent could kill an elf with the right blade. For Blanc LaBelle, his weakness was nostalgia.

As the world outside his office changed, LaBelle did his best to keep his space a consistent anchor in the tides of time. His desk was made out of old oak with a mechanical typewriter where most contemporary investigators would keep a computer. He had a few pencils, some loose-leaf paper, and a small bell that looked like it should belong on a concierge desk. A pair of wooden chairs faced LaBelle's desk so that clients had to look him in the eye while talking to him. A bookshelf within reach had what looked like a full set of encyclopedias from 1977, but looking behind the covers would reveal pages of spells and rituals much older than the late seventies. The radio in his office only played jazz: instrumental masters and big band ensembles that had secured their immortality in the volumes of human culture. As the world around his office changed with pillars of steel and glass, LaBelle remained the same.

Blanc LaBelle was a thin, tall man with thick dark hair. He could have passed for forty with an easy smile and laugh lines under his forest-green eyes. Small scars from long healed wounds dotted his pale skin with a thousand stories like the constellations of the night sky. The gray suit he wore today matched the other ten that were in his closet since he never needed to wear anything else. His hands were clean and neat with an iron ring wrapped around his right ring finger. A leather holster was strapped around his chest beneath the jacket, but LaBelle never kept a firearm. Instead, he stored a small leather book about the size of his palm and a thin wand of oak wrapped with strips of dark brown leather at the handle. The tree that the wand was made from had been struck by lightning and the wood still hummed with power.

The secret to beating nostalgia was, in LaBelle's opinion, habit and routine. He always came in first thing in the morning, used his cellphone—the one concession he allowed for the 21st century—to communicate with clients from the previous day, and enjoyed a few hours of quiet work over a bagel sandwich from Dolly's diner in his office before the stockbrokers from across the hall arrived. Assuming he didn't have any clients coming in, he would leave at noon for lunch at Dolly's, then hit the streets to check for leads. Vampires and warlocks had cheating partners, fairies were always suspicious of their neighbors, and a goblin or a harpy always managed to be spotted in

22

Winstead Park. Occasionally, a high-priority job would have LaBelle out of the office for days at a time, but he rarely took those anymore. Once he got back to the office around three, LaBelle would tie up any spell work he felt the day required. At six, he'd stop by Dolly's for dinner and then go back to his apartment to prepare for the next day. Routine was the only antidote to so much change.

LaBelle had just finished his breakfast sandwich when his secretary Irene flew in. The fairy settled on the desk, only about as tall as LaBelle's coffee cup.

"Morning, Irene," LaBelle said, setting his newspaper aside. "How was your weekend?"

"Almost got buzzed with a bug zapper," Irene said, flapping her wings with a little shiver. "Still, the bacchanal was a grand success. Thank you for giving me the long weekend."

"Who am I to deny a fairy a bacchanal?" LaBelle waved a dismissive hand. "I was following up a lead on Monday and it didn't seem fair to keep you here. You see your kin so rarely these days."

"Still, thank you," Irene curtsied before switching to business. "You have two clients."

"Really?" LaBelle leaned back and checked the paper calendar on the wall. "I didn't think we'd have anyone until next week."

"Walk-ins," Irene said. "They're on the run from the Oak Hand."

LaBelle sighed and folded up his paper. "Better send them in. I'd hate for them to have made the trip for nothing."

Irene nodded and took off again, bolting through the mail slot in the door. Another moment passed and the door opened for two teenagers. The boy had dark skin and dark, curly hair. He was nervously fidgeting with the tie of a grocery store apron and his eyes darted around the room. The girl was ghostly pale with a blonde bun, covering her mouth with a white face mask and wearing a bright, yellow raincoat a size too big. LaBelle stood and brushed a few crumbs from his breakfast off his desk.

"Have a seat," LaBelle motioned to the wooden chairs. "Feel free to take off your masks. We're all friends here."

"Well, I'm—" Matt started, but struggled with the words.

"Matt helped me get here," Mira said, "but he's human."

"Well the virus doesn't infect Underfolk, so he won't catch it from us," LaBelle said. "If you don't mind, I prefer to see people face-to-face when I'm dealing with our business. It makes you easier to read."

Matt glanced over to Mira. She nodded and they both took off their masks. LaBelle was unsurprised with a human in his office, but Mira's lower tusks caught his attention.

"You're half-troll?"

"My mother was in the Copper Tooth Clan."

"I've had good relations with the Copper Tooth Clan. The roslah, Tokron, is an old friend of mine."

"Tokron isn't the roslah," Mira corrected. "His brother, Dural, has always led us. Tokron is the roslah for the Brass Ring Clan."

"Very good," LaBelle grinned. "I needed to be sure. The Oak Hand has been getting more clever, so I've had to work harder catching their lies. Prosthetics have improved a lot over the last few decades."

"Decades?" Matt asked. "How old are you?"

"Old enough to know you're in over your head," LaBelle pointed at him. "I'm sure she appreciates what you've risked, but your part in this is done."

"I should see this through. I've already lost my job for this, I might as well know how this ends."

"Kid—"

"Matt. And her name is Mira."

"Apologies," LaBelle raised his hands in surrender. "Matt, you've only just started to scrape the surface of this world. I can get Mira to safety, but you need to get out of this before you get yourself killed. You can still pretend you don't know anything, but the longer you stay, the more vulnerable you'll be to the Oak Hand or worse."

"I'm staying," Matt said, firmly.

LaBelle scratched his chin for a minute, considering the situation. Surprisingly, he chuckled. "It seems you picked up a stray, Mira. We'll have to get you back to your clan before you get him killed."

"I can't go back," Mira said. "My mother is dead. As a halfbreed, I am contesting my bonds to the clan. That's why I came to the Above. I need to find my father."

"I'm sorry for your loss," LaBelle sighed and laced his fingers on his desk. "Well, that is an interesting wrinkle in your situation. Finding human parents, especially when the child is as old as you, is never easy. If you don't know anything about him, finding him will be extremely difficult."

"Point of curiosity," Matt raised a hand. "Seeing as how I'm not fully caught up with the rest of the class, can someone explain to me how a half-troll is even possible? Did Mira's father know?"

"There's the possibility he didn't," LaBelle shrugged. "Depending on how well connected Mira's mother was, she could have had a glamour to hide her face. Alternatively, her father might not have cared —unlikely, but stranger pairings have existed in history. Mira is hardly the first half-human being to wander around the Under."

"My mother had a glamour," Mira affirmed, "she was an explorer for our clan."

"Well, an elf or a vampire, I could understand," Matt said, "but a troll?"

LaBelle scoffed and shook his head. "How typically human to only see the physical. I'm sure you didn't mean any offense, but thinking like that? It's poisonous, Matt."

"He's still adjusting," Mira said, casting a quick look at Matt.

"I'm very old, Mira," LaBelle said, scratching his ear. "I can see when someone is projecting their hopes onto someone else. You want your father to accept you, but Matt here is exactly the problem with humans these days. They only trust what their eyes see."

"Look," Matt said, "I've had thirty minutes to learn that magic and trolls are real. Maybe I'm not completely ready to dive in, but it's something I'm involved with now. I want to help Mira."

"That's not up to you," LaBelle said.

"I trust him," Mira said. "He could have run or made my situation worse, but he helped me only because I asked."

LaBelle thought for a minute, but eventually sighed and leaned closer to the pair. "Here's the deal: he can stay, but he's your responsibility when it comes to the Under. If I'm helping you find your dad, I don't have time to babysit him. And once we find your dad, Matt's no longer my problem. Agreed?"

"Agreed," Mira said. "So, where do we start?"

"Tell you what," LaBelle said, pulling an antique coin out of his desk drawer. "There's a diner a block down the road. It'll look empty, but there are folks there who can get you a bite to eat. I'll come find you after I've made a quick call."

"Shouldn't we stay here and talk, too?" Mira asked.

"No," LaBelle said, firmly. "I need to talk with some people who don't like flies on the wall. It might be easier to get what I need if they don't know everyone involved."

Chapter 3

The diner was a small establishment with dusty windows and a battered 'Closed' sign. From what Matt could tell, the diner had been closed since before the quarantine killed many of the local businesses on this street. There were visible cobwebs in the windows and everything inside looked gray and unsaturated.

"You think he sent us on a wild goose chase?" Matt asked.

"If anything should be taken from today," Mira said. "It's that nothing is as it seems." Mira walked up to the door and looked in the window, trying to peer around the closed sign. She tugged at the handle a little but stepped away when it didn't open. "Then again, I could be wrong."

"Wait," Matt said, "let me see that coin."

Mira reached into the pocket of her raincoat and dug around for the metal disk LaBelle had given her. Instead of a face or ancient building, both sides of the coin had a symbol of a square, triangle, and circle all linked together. Matt compared the coin's size to the lock just below the handle. "Nothing is as it seems? Then I bet this isn't for paying."

Matt maneuvered the token into the key slot and it slipped through, followed by a distinct click. Mira pulled the handle again and the door opened easily. As he stepped through the threshold, Matt felt something drop into his right pocket. He reached in and pulled out the same coin he'd just used to unlock the door.

Inside, the restaurant was a stark contrast to the exterior. The drab ghost of a diner had been replaced by something vibrant and alive. The booths had red vinyl cushions and red tables that glittered a little from within. The floor was a familiar black and white checkerboard pattern Matt had seen in diners all his life. Opposite the entry door was a staircase that led up to another level of the building. To the left of the stairway was an old-fashioned pay phone and on the right was what looked like a manhole cover with a steel handle. Along the walls were signed pictures, but Matt noticed that they were all portraits of wizards, centaurs, and other fantasy creatures rather than human celebrities. Matt smelled bacon cooking and heard the sound of silverware against plates over the din of conversation.

"Take a seat," a woman's voice said. "There's plenty to choose from. And no need for the masks in here. We got nothing to hide"

Matt stared as the woman walked by, carrying a tray of eggs, toast, and fruit. She was in her thirties with dark skin and dark hair tied into a braid that went down between her shoulders. Matt looked down and watched the woman's horse legs step through the diner, her hooves sharply clicking against the tile. The centaur waitress stopped at a table of young people with vines mixed into their hair and moss growing on their skin in patterns like tattoos. At the counter, two fairies were splitting a pancake and one got her foot momentarily stuck in a stray puddle of syrup. Mira took Matt's arm and led him away from the counter. They sat and Mira shoved a menu into Matt's hand.

"Will you stop staring?" Mira snapped.

"Are those elves?" Matt asked, hiding behind the menu. "Like, wood elves?"

"No, those are dryads," Mira said, taking her raincoat off and bunching it beside her in the booth.

"What's a dryad?"

"Snobs," Mira shrugged. "They're kinda rude, at least to trolls. Well, at least to me, but no one is nice to me."

"Why?"

"I'm half-human," Mira said. "That makes me half the enemy."

"Do all Underfolk hate humans that much?"

"It kinda varies, but there's a reason so few of us live in the Above. To the fae, humans are playthings that break too easily. To the magi, they are uneasy allies they need to sidestep around to help. And to the rest of us, humans are hunters or prey. It depends on what kind of history you have with humanity."

"I guess I should start taking notes," Matt said before looking down at the menu.

The centaur waitress came over to their table and grinned. She took a pad from her apron and pulled her pen out from behind her ear. "What can I get started for you two?"

"Can I get…" Mira said, considering the menu, "three pancakes, bacon, two eggs scrambled, a grilled cheese, a cheeseburger with no tomatoes, a corn muffin, a side of fries, three whole oranges, and a glass of milk?"

"Got it," the waitress said, punctuating the completed order with a tap of her pen. "How about you?"

"Uh," Matt stammered, trying not to get distracted by some of the stranger offerings on the menu, "french fries and a vanilla milkshake?"

"Sure thing. You want a Witch Hazel Shot?"

"What's a—?"

"No," Mira urged. "No thank you."

The waitress nodded and walked back toward the kitchen at a slow trot. Mira leaned forward and picked at her left tusk. "Sorry," Mira said, a little embarrassed. " Last I had to eat was scraps from yesterday's dinner."

"What was yesterday's dinner?"

"The clan had fish and onions. I got what was left."

"Huh," Matt nodded, folding his arms on the table and looking around.

"Are you OK?" Mira asked. "I bet this is a lot to take in at once."

"It's weird, but not in a bad way," Matt began. "There's things that feel familiar and things that feel so strange. We're in a diner getting french fries and pancakes, but there are dryads and fairies. If we take away the Dungeons and Dragons nonsense, it feels just like people."

"Trolls aren't exactly held in the highest esteem in pop culture," Mira noted. "Maybe it's better if you meet centaurs and trolls in real life rather than just in the movies."

"What I'm trying to say is that this doesn't feel as weird as it should. It's a lot to digest, but I think I'm open to learning about it."

"You don't have to stay. You got me where you promised."

"I'm too curious to go back now," Matt smiled. "I want to see this through. How am I supposed to go back to shelving soup cans after this? And to think this started with you and this…LaBelle guy."

"You kids know LaBelle?" The centaur waitress grinned. She set down Matt's milkshake, Mira's milk, and a plate of oranges on the table. "I can't help but wonder what that man has gotten himself into now."

"Do you know him?" Matt asked. "We just met him today."

"He's a regular here. Comes in first thing in the morning for a breakfast sandwich, then comes back for lunch and dinner. He always orders black coffee with steak and eggs. A bit of a loner, but he never starts a fight he can't finish. Keeps the trouble outside, if you know what I mean."

"If you don't mind me asking," Mira said, rolling an orange in her hands. "Is he trustworthy? I don't really have any references besides secondhand stories."

"Ask anyone in the Fold."

"The Fold?" Mira asked.

"You're an Under kid, huh? Well, the Fold is kind of a running joke: the Above meets the Under, so you 'fold' it. Anyone from the Under who lives in the Above tends to consider themselves all part of the same community, no matter which faction they come from. And, while he'd never admit it, LaBelle is at the center of the Fold in Hedgefield."

"Do you trust him, Miss—?" Matt started.

"Oh, please," the centaur laughed. "Don't call me Miss. It makes me feel older than two hundred. Just call me Dolly."

"Well, Dolly, how do we know we can trust LaBelle?"

"He's been a constant fixture up here," Dolly said. "He helps Underfolk hide when they're in danger, he gets them to others in the community, and he finds a place for them here."

"Sounds like you have some experience," Mira said.

"Before I came up," Dolly nodded sadly, "my sister was abducted by the Oak Hand when she was just a foal. I disobeyed the Fae Queen's order and came up looking for her. LaBelle helped me get her back down to the Under. I stayed here afterward, but LaBelle has always been my friend in the Above."

"So, no one knows who he is?" Matt asked. "He just popped up one day and started solving people's problems?"

"Quite the opposite," Dolly said. "Underfolk in the Fold just turned to him for help one day and he was decent enough to do something. If he's helping you? I wouldn't look a gift horse in the mouth."

"Was that a pun?" Matt asked.

The waitress laughed and walked away. Matt looked at Mira and took a sip of his milkshake. Mira only shrugged and took a sip of her milk before biting into her first orange like an apple.

"Irene?" LaBelle called from his office. The mail slot clicked open and the fairy darted into the room. LaBelle smiled as she landed on his desk. "No calls for the next hour, please."

"If anyone calls, can I say why?"

"I leave that up to your discretion. I need to discuss Mira's case with the Council."

"I hope they're in a good mood."

"Knowing what the dragons think about me? I can't afford to wait for them to be in a good mood. No calls from anyone."

"Understood," Irene nodded and fluttered back through the mail slot to her watch post.

LaBelle opened his desk drawer and took out a leather pouch with a star on the front flap. Rolling his neck, LaBelle opened the packet and took out a small, triangular leaf. With the tip of his finger, LaBelle hit the plunger on the desk bell and listened to the tone resonate through his office. He licked his lips and exhaled before carefully setting the leaf on his tongue. LaBelle closed his eyes, leaned back in his chair, and took a few slow breaths. Each exhale he took made him feel heavier and slower as if each inhale was filling his awareness with thick cotton. The clock ticking in his office slowed until LaBelle couldn't hear it anymore and he was left to sit in silence. His mind drifted from feeling until his awareness slipped away from his physical body.

"LaBelle," a soft voice said. "I'm surprised you called us here."

LaBelle opened his eyes and looked up at the young woman standing above him. She had a large twist of dark dreadlocks hanging down her shoulders and black skin. The curve of her smile shined like a sliver of moon in the night sky. Her eyes were a deep brown that reminded LaBelle of liquid bronze in a glowing forge. The sky above her was bright blue and LaBelle could feel the tickle of grass on his face as a breeze brought the spectral field to life.

"Aili," LaBelle stood up and grinned. "It's always so nice to see you here."

"If that were true, you'd come visit the Under more often. Have you found something more captivating in the Above and failed to tell me? It's been so long since you contacted me, so I was surprised by your summons."

"I apologize for calling the meeting so abruptly. I need to talk to the Council immediately."

"Immediately?" Aili said, feigning shock. "Well, we should call them together if the great Blanc LaBelle requires us!"

"I didn't mean to offend," LaBelle said, holding up his hands in apology. "I simply wanted to express the urgency."

The Realm of the Council changed slowly as LaBelle walked through the environment. Aili strolled by LaBelle's side, her bare feet padding against the carpet of grass that shifted after they walked a few feet from where LaBelle had woken. The world turned from grassy pastures to an arid desert to dense woods and other biomes that clashed and washed through the realm in waves. After they walked through the unreal space for a while, Aili and LaBelle stopped in a stone ruin with glowing stained glass windows of the six Great Dragons, the four Magi Prima, and the Fae Queen. Beneath the mosaic of the dragons was a flat, wide platform, but the glass portraits of the Magi Prima and the Fae Queen each had a stone podium for them to stand behind during the session.

"No matter how often I come," LaBelle said, "I always find this place so marvelous."

"I'm pleased to know I can still surprise you after all this time," Aili said. "It's refreshing that my taste hasn't soured over the years."

"How much longer until the Council arrives? I understand the short notice, but—"

"They'll be ready," Aili assured him, taking a step onto the sands of a beach as the realm shifted under her feet. "You know how strange time works in this place. Before you ever asked—"

"—we were already here."

LaBelle turned quickly in the space and looked up. Extoran was ancient, even by LaBelle's standards. The dark blue dragon was considered the king of the dragons, a title earned only by those brave enough to fight for it. The giant reptile was the size of a double-decker bus with his dark wings spread out behind him like a cape of scales. His crown of horns almost doubled the size of Extoran's head, which was already the size of a minivan. On either side of the dragon king were five other dragons: red, green, onyx, ivory, and gold.

"Extoran," LaBelle said, holding his head high, "you humble me with your magnificence."

"Praise rings hollow from my destined destroyer."

"Don't tell me you're sore about that prophecy."

"You may scoff at my death, LaBelle," the ancient dragon rumbled, "but if you are prophesied to end my life? I intend to remain cynical of your sweet words."

"Why sour a compliment with distrust, Extoran?" A woman's voice said, lyrically.

LaBelle turned and bowed deeply to the Fae Queen. She was incredibly beautiful with long, dark tresses that framed her delicate face. LaBelle had heard that each person who looked upon the Fae Queen saw something different, but it was always how they interpreted beauty at that moment. These days, LaBelle saw a woman with slim and angular features, thin lips, and eyes as dark as the stormy sea. Pastel blues, greens, and pinks streaked her pale skin like an aurora borealis across a full moon. Her brow was adorned with a crown of roses, lilies, and daisies with bees and a hummingbird fluttering between each flower. Her dress was the color of sea foam and flowed around her body as if she had turned a wave into a fitted gown.

"Your Majesty," LaBelle smiled, rising from his bow after an appropriate time. "I am—as always—privileged with your company."

"LaBelle, LaBelle," the Fae Queen laughed. "You are almost as old as I am and I have yet to meet anyone else with your manners."

"Flattery is not manners," Extoran snarled. "LaBelle ensnares you with his charms."

"Charm is something I can appreciate," the Fae Queen purred. "At least LaBelle has some sense of decorum."

The blue dragon growled and glared at the Fae Queen. In response, she laughed and waved a hand dismissively.

"Now, now, Extoran," Aili said, walking up to the last empty podium. "You don't need to be rude. The Magi Prima has always had a successful working relationship with Blanc LaBelle."

"He's a scoundrel and a knave," Extoran grumbled. "And were it not for the protections granted by other members of the Council? I would have rid us of that pest decades ago."

"There's no need for violence." An old man with a long white beard appeared on the dais with Aili, opening an ancient leather book on the podium and taking out a pen. The Magi Scriptum chuckled as he started notes for the council session. "Not that it would do you much good in this literal meeting of the minds."

Two other magi joined the Magi Prima at their space in the meeting: a man with gray dreadlocks and a beard and a woman with red hair and pale green eyes. LaBelle suddenly felt like he'd been dropped down several feet lower as the platforms of the Council loomed over him. LaBelle didn't mind if it made them more comfortable speaking with him.

"Now then," Aili smiled, folding her hands on the podium, "what is so important that you have called us together, Blanc LaBelle?"

Chapter 4

"Council," LaBelle began, pacing the chamber. "By my summons, I came to speak with you seeking your wisdom. I need to once again ask special permissions to reveal the world of magic to a human."

"Why?" the Fae Queen asked, perching her chin in her palm. LaBelle always appreciated how the fairy woman would cut straight to the heart of the matter. No trick questions or dancing around the elephant in the room, just the blunt truth of what she needed to know. He'd known the Fae Queen for too long to waste either of their time avoiding the obvious questions.

"Without any direct breach of privacy," LaBelle began, looking between the Fae Queen and the Magi Prima, "my client is half-human. She is in the Above seeking her father."

Extoran snarled deeply, raising his upper lip. "Humans should not mix with our world. Once they discover our existence, alliances like the Oak Hand follow. Less than two thousand years ago, dragons could fearlessly soar in the skies. Now, the handful of us that remain have been forced to hide in sewers and remote caves. We were all hunted to near extinction and the fewer humans that know of our existence is better for the safety of all Underfolk. Humans have no place in the Under!"

"The evidence of this child," the Fae Queen said, amused, "suggests otherwise. What is her connection?"

"Half-troll," LaBelle said. "From the clans that are right under Hedgefield."

"I've seen half-trolls before," Aili said. "A troll and a human is an odd union, but not unheard of. Oftentimes, their children struggle to live with their troll clans and have the natural urge to find their human families. What does her mother say about this?"

"Her mother is dead," LaBelle said. "My client wants her father to claim blood ties."

"She has blood ties to her clan!" Extoran growled. While some of the other dragons looked sympathetic to LaBelle's story, the king of the dragons maintained a stern stance when it came to humans. The dragon's heart could not be moved by words, or at least not LaBelle's words.

"I would keep her interactions limited," LaBelle assured them. "Only one human would have to learn about our world and the half-troll would be introduced gradually into the Above. Anyone else involved will have their memory wiped."

"Too many risks," the wizard with dreadlocks shook his head. "Any time that a human is brought into the Under too soon—"

"A poor sampling is not an indicator for the whole," The Fae Queen said.

"Easy for you to say," Extoran growled. "You treat humans as prey, fairy. Most of us still view them as predators."

"That was ages ago," Aili said, "so long ago that even some Underfolk living in the Above consider dragons nothing but a myth."

"We are all that is left!" Extoran growled. "This is the danger of dropping humans into our world. They will hunt and destroy what they don't understand! The Great Dragons vote to refuse your request, LaBelle!"

"Let me make a further case," LaBelle said, looking up at the blue dragon sternly. There was some discomfort from Extoran, but he recoiled slightly and folded his wings tight against his body. LaBelle bowed his head to the towering dragon and looked back to the others. Once Extoran was placated, the rest of the Council seemed more at ease.

"We have always been at odds with mankind," LaBelle continued. "I knew this well before any of the Great Dragons were hatched. The only one here older than me is the Fae Queen herself, long may she reign. I was there when the agreements between humans and Underfolk were made. I shook hands with the human leaders to seal the Under Pact. The Magi Prima have consulted me on their dealings with the Above more often than I have consulted them. I turn to the Council to ask for your blessing. Without it, my work will become vastly more difficult."

"Should that be a concern for the Council?" Aili asked. "Do you intend to act without our permission?"

"The purpose of this Council," LaBelle started, "the reason your factions agreed to this alliance—is the protection of all Underfolk. And that includes my client. Without parentage, she could be at the mercy of her clan. At best, she'll be a social pariah. At worst? Well, we know that trolls aren't known for their charitable attitudes."

"Get to the point, LaBelle," Extoran grumbled.

"We are talking about someone who is trapped between worlds. The trolls only tolerated her for this long because of her blood ties. Without her mother, she won't be safe in the clan she grew up in. She won't be accepted by another clan or any other place in the Under, not truly. I need to find somewhere for her to live safely, with or without her father. I'll handle any clean-up if things go wrong. I'm asking for the chance to give her a home. I won't just pass her over to the first human I find. I'll follow all the troll laws and rites. You have my word, bound by magic older than anyone in this room."

The Council shared a few looks back and forth. The dragons rumbled to one another in low purrs, a tongue that even LaBelle couldn't understand. There were a few whispers from the Magi Prima and the Fae Queen had the sternest face she could muster as she considered the matter privately.

"I say we allow LaBelle to do his investigation," the Fae Queen said after the Council spoke among themselves for a while. "We do have the responsibility to all those in our care, no matter how much magic is in their blood."

"Agreed," Aili said, nodding to the other Magi Prima. "We need this done in a way that will ensure the secrecy and safety of the Under. LaBelle is best suited for this task."

"The Great Dragons think it is foolish," Extoran snarled, "but we would rather hold LaBelle accountable for what he plans to do either way. Mind your place, LaBelle. I've never eaten an immortal before."

"Your conditions couldn't be clearer," LaBelle bowed and looked to each person in the Council Realm. "As the one who called us here, I adjourn this meeting."

The Great Dragons unfolded their wings and flew off first, fading into the storm that had brewed behind them to exit the realm with Extoran at their lead. The Fae Queen dissolved away in the winds kicked up by the wingbeats of the dragons. Most of the Magi Prima slowly stepped down from their dais and disappeared into the wall behind the podium. With a single step away from the dais, Aili and LaBelle were on even ground again.

"You're treading less carefully before the king of the dragons."

"Extoran doesn't like cowardice," LaBelle said, walking to Aili. "And I was more confident with the Fae Queen."

"And the Magi Prima?"

"I figured I'd earned your trust after all this time," LaBelle said, adjusting his hat. "The magi owed me that much."

"This…half-troll girl," Aili said. "Is she worth it?"

"Worth what?"

"Worth having the risk of Extoran swallowing you in two bites?"

"I like to think I'd put up a good fight and make it three bites."

"Be careful, LaBelle. I like you, but others are looking for a reason to take you down. Take care of this girl. I think she's more important than you realize."

"I promise, Aili. Getting her to her father is my top priority."

###

Mira folded the last bite of her final pancake into thirds and pushed it into her mouth, took her cup of syrup, and drank it in a quick slurp. She leaned back in the booth and swallowed the last mouthful. Mira let out a satisfied breath and reached out to take a couple of french fries off one of her plates. She looked up and noticed Matt watching her with an amused smile.

"Sorry," Mira grinned, wiping her face with a napkin. "Believe it or not, that was actually pretty polite for troll eating."

"You've never seen high school boys at the lunch table," Matt laughed.

"Blanc!" The waitress smiled as the bell over the door rang. "Always a regular pleasure. Steak and eggs?"

"Medium-well and scrambled, thanks, Dolly," LaBelle said, taking off his hat. He walked over to where the teens were sitting, motioned for Matt to move further into the booth, and sat across from Mira.

"I just finished talking to the Council."

"Wait…the Council-Council?" Mira asked.

"This is about introducing a human to the world of Underfolk. Did you really think the Council wouldn't be involved?"

"Who's the council?" Matt asked.

"The Under Council," LaBelle said. "They oversee the governance of all the Underfolk. I had to convince them to let me take Mira's case since it means interacting with humans."

"Where does that put me?" Matt asked.

"When we find Mira's father? I'm going to wipe your memory of everything you've seen and send you home. You'll think it was all just a fever dream after a bad bout with the virus that's going around."

"Is that a threat?"

"I could do a lot worse than wipe your memory, Matt."

"Mr. LaBelle," Mira said, "Matt's my friend and—"

"And if the Council finds out he knows about our world, you're putting him in more danger than anything I could claim to do. They barely want me to talk to your father. I can allow him to stay with you for moral support. Once you're with your family, he's going to have to forget. Understand?"

"You said family, not father," Matt said.

LaBelle sighed and scratched his chin. "In cases like this? It's not unusual that parents aren't always found. Or, if they are found, they don't want anything to do with their Under children. That's why I don't want Mira projecting her hopes onto you. There's no guarantee that her father will be prepared to take her in. If that's the case? We'll have to take Mira back to the trolls."

"But I don't want to go back to my clan!"

"That may not be your choice," LaBelle said. "If I can't track down your father, your mother was blood bound to your clan. I have to honor that connection by troll law."

"That's not fair!" Mira snapped, hitting the table. "I don't want to go back to the clan!"

"Settle down, Mira," LaBelle hushed her, looking around to make sure no one in the diner was too disturbed by the outburst. "There's no point in getting worked up. I will try and get you to your father. However, you have to prepare for the possibility that you'll have to go back to your clan."

"Can't I stay up here anyway?"

"You're sixteen," LaBelle said. "You need to be with your family."

Mira folded her arms and slumped back in the booth. "I thought you were going to help me find my dad."

"I will if I can," LaBelle said, "but you need to realize that there might not be the happy ending you're hoping for. Understand?"

Mira nodded, though it was clearly only out of understanding, not acceptance. LeBelle took her reluctant agreement at face value. "Do you have somewhere to stay?"

"Not really," Mira confessed. "I was hoping we'd find my dad before tonight."

"I see you've done about as much planning as I'd expected," LaBelle said, amused. He turned and looked up at the centaur waitress as she came over with his plate. "Dolly? Do you have any openings upstairs?"

"Looking to make a deal, LaBelle?" Dolly grinned.

"I know better than to enter a fae deal so recklessly. Call it a favor for a friend."

"We got a couple spare beds," the centaur waitress said. "Why? You trying to get away from Irene for a few days?"

"Dolly, this is my client, Mira."

"We met," Dolly said. "I didn't know you were taking new cases. I almost didn't believe them."

"Well, I had to try before turning her away heartlessly," LaBelle smirked. "She just needs somewhere to stay for a few days while I'm working her case. I'll swing by in the morning to talk to her over a late breakfast so you won't lose her for the rush."

Dolly considered Mira carefully and nodded. "If you're willing to do a little work in the diner, I don't see a problem. As long as LaBelle doesn't take you away during breakfast and has you back for dishes after the dinner rush? I think we can come to an arrangement."

"I've always wanted to try some real baking," Mira offered, "if I can help with that."

"Perfect! Daryl always needs another hand in the kitchen."

"Thank you," Mira nodded. "I'll do whatever you need me to so I can be useful."

"We'll get you workin' first thing in the morning," Dolly said, putting a hand on Mira's shoulder. She glanced over at Matt and furrowed her brow. "You're a funny-lookin' elf, aren't you?"

Matt swallowed his mouthful of milkshake and looked at Mira and LaBelle. "I'm, uh…not an elf."

"He's part-magi," LaBelle responded calmly to Matt's panic. "His grandmother is a Salem Descendant and she had Matt help get Mira to me. No magic in him, I'm afraid, but he knows enough to help Mira around the Above. He's got a foot in each world, so to speak."

"Never hurts to have a friend on the other side," Dolly agreed. "Well, as long as he keeps his nose clean and doesn't bring any trouble? That'll be fine. And, sweetie? Next time somebody asks if you're an elf? Just say yes."

Dolly chuckled and walked back over to the counter. LaBelle reached into his coat pocket and handed Matt a small, green seedpod. "Swallow that."

"Why?" Matt asked, looking at the legume.

"Insurance. If you're gonna split your time between our world and yours, that'll keep you from running your mouth off. It's temporary and it'll end as soon as you pass it—that'll hurt, by the way, so you'll know when you need a new dose."

"Is this necessary?" Matt asked. "I won't tell anyone. No one would believe me."

"The alternative is I wipe your memory and you forget this ever happened. If you want to stay and help Mira? That's the cost."

Matt looked at the seedpod with some concern. He took a deep breath and stuffed the green thing into his mouth. He swallowed it like a capsule, gagging a little as he choked it down. He took a big sip of his milkshake and showed his empty mouth to the detective. "I'm all in."

LaBelle shook his head and doused his eggs in hot sauce. "Your friend is gonna get you in trouble."

"It's my first time in the Above as a half-troll," Mira shrugged, piercing a stray pickle with a toothpick from her earlier cheeseburger, "trouble is something I'm used to already."

Chapter 5

Matt's drive home was quieter, the usual bumper-to-bumper traffic thinned by the statewide "Stay at Home" orders. Normally, driving from downtown at this time of day would take forty-five minutes or more in the gridlock. With so few people leaving their homes, Matt was able to make the same drive in twenty. Leaving his car in the designated spot by the curb, Matt unlocked his front door and walked up the stairs to the second level of his family's duplex.

The top level of the duplex was a kitchenette that doubled as a living space, a bathroom down the hall, Matt's room, and his parents' bedroom. Mr. and Mrs. Brand had owned half of the duplex since they got married and covered the walls with pictures from their days of globetrotting before Matt was born: China, South Africa, Australia, France, Brazil, and everywhere in between. Matt's mom had been a travel writer when she met his dad, a commercial pilot. They kept meeting at airport bars and—if Matt was to believe the stories—they traveled the world together for the months leading up to Matt's dad proposing mid-flight.

"Hey, Matt," Matt's mother called, sitting on the couch and looking over a tablet screen, "how was work?"

Audrey Brand's long, black hair was tied into a ponytail and her stylish glasses sat on the bridge of her slender nose. She had a bright smile and dark brown eyes. With her globetrotting done, for now, Matt's mom was a feature writer for the local papers and a few of her articles hit national news sites in the past couple of years.

"It was interesting. I'm kinda tired, so I think I'm gonna call it a night."

"You don't want any supper? I was gonna order pizza again. Support small business and all that."

"Maybe in a bit," Matt said. "I'm gonna go wash up. Work was brutal today."

"Good! Gotta keep healthy!" Mrs. Brand reminded him as Matt walked to his room.

Closing the door behind him, Matt dropped his backpack on his bed and exhaled. He had survived his first day in the Fold, but Matt knew it was only a matter of time before he had to decide between Mira and his Above life. He wasn't sure if he should be getting a new job now or if Blanc LaBelle was as good as everyone seemed to think he was. Matt had already texted Jake, explaining he wouldn't be coming in tomorrow morning because the doctor wouldn't have the test results before then. It was a believable lie and Matt told himself this was more important.

After a quick shower, Matt went back to his room and opened his laptop. He did a few quick web searches for anything about Underfolk, trolls, fairies, or anything else that he'd encountered today. After a deep dive, all he found were old legends and myths or Hollywood special effects videos. Looking up the Oak Hand led to very few resources, except for a few loose threads on various social sites. One of the pages was a sign-up page for some kind of newsletter, but it felt more like recruitment to Matt. Paranoid, he cleared his browser history and did his best to cover his tracks after examining the questionable webpage.

Matt was organizing his thoughts for the day when his mom came in with a few slices of pizza. "Can't let you go to bed hungry. My mother would never let me hear the end of it."

"Thanks, Mom," Matt smiled. He set his pen aside and took a bite of warm pizza.

"What's this?" Mrs. Brand asked, pointing to Matt's laptop. A tab was still open about legends from Norway and an illustration of a monstrous troll dominated half the page.

"Research," Matt said. He didn't want to lie, but he didn't know if now was the time to test LaBelle's seedpod. "It's for a story I'm thinking of writing."

"You'll have to let me read it when it's ready," Mrs. Brand smiled. "I always liked your stories. How was work?"

"It was busy. People are still treating things like the end of the world or business as normal with no in-between."

"Things are just getting wilder and weirder," Matt's mom said. "And they're working you poor kids to the bone! God knows this wasn't what you signed up for when you applied for the stockroom."

"I'll live," Matt shrugged. "At least I don't have to do school work on top of this for another few months."

"Small blessings. I have to get back to work myself. I'm in the middle of a story about the state enforcing new mask policies. You working late tomorrow?"

"Probably. I'll be home around eight."

"These long days. I don't know how you do it."

"Beats the graveyard shift," Matt said. "I don't think that crew sees anyone outside of the store these days."

"Well, don't work too late. There's no use in beating yourself up when your boss refuses to give you a raise."

"Yeah, but who needs a raise if they leave free candy bars in the break room?"

Matt's mom laughed and closed the door behind her on the way out. Matt took another bite of pizza, set his plate aside, and leaned back in his chair. He had been playing catch-up all day, but there was still one big question he needed to answer. Matt rolled his shoulders and approached his laptop again.

"Alright," Matt said, taking another bite of pizza before typing. "Blanc…LaBelle…detective."

The first result was an article about private eyes followed by a list of police reports that didn't seem like they should be connected. Matt spent the next two hours reading about Blanc LaBelle doing everything from solving murders to freeing misidentified convicts. The cases went back ten years, then twenty, then thirty. By the time Matt's pizza had gone cold, there were cases about a detective named Blanc LaBelle from over a hundred years ago. His exploits went all over the world, from France to Australia, the Caribbean, and the Americas. Pictures of him were rare, and the few that did pop up were always out of focus or otherwise unclear. He wasn't famous by any stretch and the cases were far enough apart in time and distance that most people would just think it was a coincidence. LaBelle appeared to be one of those people who was most talented at blending into the background of the world. It was like Mira had said, *only if you're looking for it.*

Then again, Matt mused, *maybe he's just got a lot of those seedpods for everyone he meets.*

Matt closed his laptop and flopped onto the bed, trying to process everything that had happened. He started his day at the grocery store and now a whole second world existed just beneath his real life. A world of centaurs and fairies, trolls and lost children. Matt wondered if there was a house under his house and the thought made his mind swim as to what could be living right beneath him.

His phone vibrated on his desk and Matt got up to check it. The number didn't look familiar and the message looked less familiar.

<<How bare his kfoing?>>

<<What?>> Matt texted back.

There was a long pause and Matt waited while the three dots popped slowly on his screen. Finally, the number called and Matt begrudgingly answered.

"Hello?"

"Matt? Is that you? Sorry, I've never used one of these before."

"Who is this?"

"Oh! It's Mira. Sorry, I should have led with that. Dolly had some phones for people staying here and this way I don't have to scrape together quarters for every time I want to call you."

"Remind me to teach you how to text," Matt laughed. "How are you?"

"Settling in for the night. Dolly set me up in a private room! I've never had a room to myself before. A bit empty. "

"Lonely?"

"Kinda. But I don't feel like someone is gonna roll on top of me."

"Trolls just pile together?"

"My mom and I used to share a bed. She moved a lot in her sleep."

"Can I ask you something?" Matt asked, rolling onto his back on the bed. "I've been looking up LaBelle. How do you know you can trust him? I mean, what do you know besides what we learned today?"

"He helps people out of bad situations. I don't know what your newspapers found on him, but it probably just barely covers what he's done."

"Yeah, that's why I'm worried."

"I don't have another choice. LaBelle is my best chance at getting out of the Under and away from my clan. The more time I spend in the Above, the less I care about how I stay here."

"I hope you're right. I really do. Your dad will be lucky to have you."

"Thanks, Matt. Will you come by tomorrow?"

"I think so. I told my boss I couldn't come in, so I have no other plans."

"I'll see you then. Hey, are we friends?"

"I don't see why not."

"Cool. That's two things I've never had before today: a bed to myself and a friend. So far, my trip to the Above hasn't been so bad."

"My first trip to the Under has been eventful, I'll say that. Get some sleep. I'm sure we'll have plenty more adventures tomorrow."

"Goodnight."

"Goodnight, Mira.

"Wait, Matt?"

"Yeah?"

"How do I hang up this kind of phone?"

###

LaBelle waved his hand and unlocked the door to his loft. His apartment was like his office, but with a few more embellishments that would make museum curators go wide-eyed. "Souvenirs" would be a better word, but LaBelle never got to tell anyone the stories behind each object that marked the events of his life: medals he'd earned fighting various wars for the French, the old saxophone he hadn't played since the late 40s, a sword he'd used in Greece, and a collection of wands he'd confiscated from Nazi wizards in World War II. He had a simple kitchen but never kept more than the basics on hand for the rare guest. By the front door was a bell just like the one in his office that would sometimes ring when the Council meetings were called by someone other than him, usually in the dead of night when the Above was meant to be sleeping. The loft was a testament to his life that no one would ever hear about.

Taking off his coat, LaBelle let Irene fly out of the inner pocket to the small terrarium on top of one of the bookshelves. She busied herself in the enclosure while LaBelle settled in, hanging his coat and hat on a hook behind the door, rolled up his shirtsleeves, and turned on the old radio in the corner with a wave of his wand.

LaBelle walked over to his small kitchen, separated from the living room by only a waist-high countertop. He reached into the freezer, pulled out a handful of ice, dropped it into a glass from the cabinet, and filled it with a strong, amber liquid from a bottle under the counter. Drink in hand, LaBelle went over to the couch and sat with a huff, kicking his feet up on the coffee table and leaning back so his head flopped over the top of the couch.

"Something is bothering you," Irene flew down and stood on the tip of LaBelle's shoe. "You don't break out the liquor until Friday unless you're having a bad week."

"It's irritating that you know my habits that well." LaBelle tilted his head down to look at her.

"What can I say? You're an open book once someone bothers to learn the language. What's on your mind, boss?"

"You're not my shrink, Irene."

"Well, clearly you need one. Something is bothering you. Is it the girl?"

"If you're so smart," LaBelle said, shaking Irene off his shoe with a wiggle of his foot, "you tell me."

"I think you're more invested in this than you let on," Irene said, fluttering down to the coffee table. "Why? We've done parentage cases like this before."

"And we saw how that went."

"Admittedly, the reaction wasn't ideal."

"Ideal?" LaBelle laughed. He stood and paced the room, taking a swig from his glass. "The woman pulled a shotgun and tried to kill her son…and me!"

"She wasn't prepared," Irene said. "He had a lot of fairy features and most humans don't know how to—"

"Exactly," LaBelle said. "Humans can't always accept our world. I don't know why Mira didn't just stay in the Under. It's not paradise, but coming Above isn't worth the risk."

"I left the Under, too," Irene said. "And I came up from a charmed life that didn't involve trolls. It wasn't my choice, but I don't know if I'd go back if I got the offer."

"I know," LaBelle sighed. He swirled the contents of his glass and took another sip. "I just don't understand why she came up here and why she got that boy involved!"

"I don't mind Matt!"

"You spoke to him for ten seconds, if that."

"He saw me for longer than that mother and her son. Give him some credit. He might be one of the good humans out there."

"The Oak Hand ruined my taste for humans a while ago," LaBelle growled. He tilted his glass into his mouth and finished his liquor. "I don't trust him. He's got no business being involved with our world."

"Still, you let him stay."

"Despite my better judgment," LaBelle said. He twirled his wrist and the glass and ice vanished. "I don't know, Irene. Something about him is different. He's too comfortable around Underfolk."

"You say that like it's a bad thing."

"Comfort comes from naivety or acceptance. And acceptance only comes from experience. I don't understand how he's so open to this after a few hours."

"So you think he's lying?"

"The Oak Hand has gotten through defenses with less than lies. Hell, a handful got into the Under with a few well-placed lies. And we're just supposed to accept that he and Mira are best friends? After a day?"

"They're children, Blanc. Children aren't as jaded as you."

"I wouldn't know." LaBelle sat on the couch again and ran his hand down his face. "I didn't tell the Council about him. That was stupid."

"I wouldn't be surprised if they already knew. What's to be done?"

"Nothing I can do," LaBelle reasoned. He stood, cracked his knuckles, and exhaled. "For now, I'm going to bed. I need to go to the Under tomorrow and learn what I can from the Copper Tooth Clan."

"Are you going to tell them you have Mira?"

"Maybe. If I do, there will be conditions. Right now, I'm just looking for any information they can give me on Mira's mother. Hell, maybe I'll surprise the kid with something from home."

"That's some compassionate thinking!" Irene praised. "In a world as big and chaotic as this, she could use something familiar for comfort."

"Then I'd better get some sleep," LaBelle said. "Turn the lights off when you're done for the night."

"As long as you leave the radio on."

LaBelle nodded and left the living room. He walked into his bedroom and took off his shirt before sitting on the bed to take off his shoes. LaBelle took off the big ring on his right hand, a rough shape of a tree that wrapped its branches around his ring finger. As he set the ring on the table, LaBelle caught sight of a gold, hoop earring on his side table from back in his pirating days. It had changed hands many times, traditionally meant to pay his funeral rites. Now, it was just a reminder that he was still here while those he knew were left behind.

Waving off the cobwebs that littered his mind, LaBelle finished getting dressed for bed and climbed under the blankets. He stretched a little, turned off the light by his bed, and blinked into the slowly changing dark that made his room look different. While the rest of the world faded to a dull, dark blue, the gold hoop shined in the darkness. Sleep didn't come easy, but it rarely did for LaBelle's troubled mind.

<u>Chapter 6</u>

Matt still had the coin that had popped back into his pocket, so he used it again when he walked into the diner the next morning. Again, the key coin popped back into his pocket after Matt crossed the doorway into the magical space. This early in the morning, the diner was a little busier and Matt could only find an open spot at the counter. The air smelled of cooked bacon and coffee while the patrons chattered over the crackle of the hot skillet.

"Hey, Matt!" Dolly clopped by with a tray of hot food. "Give me a mo' and I'll be right back."

"Actually, I just came to see if Mira—"

"She's working right now!" Dolly chided, playfully. "She can visit when we got fewer hungry folks. Now, you wait at the counter and I'll come take your order."

Matt smiled and took a look at the menu. His phone buzzed in his pocket and Matt answered.

"Hello?"

"Matt? It's Jake."

"Hey, Jake, I was just—"

"You're not here for your shift."

"Yeah, I know, but the doctors still want me to isolate until we get the test back." Matt found it was easier to lie to Jake than his mom.

"Fine, how long will it take?"

"I don't know. They just said they'd get back to me."

Jack sighed loudly on the other end of the phone. "Don't bother coming back for your shifts. Leave your apron on the loading dock and I'll send your last check in the mail."

"Jake—"

"I need reliable bodies here, not flakes and no-shows. Goodbye, Matt."

The line went dead and Matt let out a long breath. He should have been more distressed about getting fired, but the way the job had been going had made Matt consider quitting since the pandemic started. He slipped his phone back into his pocket and looked over the menu. At least now he could firmly plant his feet in one world at a time.

Dolly's loud hooves announced her coming back towards the counter and Matt turned to meet her. "Could I get the scrambled eggs and bacon?"

"You might want to order one of the muffins," Dolly suggested. "Fresh baked this morning…blueberry."

"Then I'll have a blueberry muffin, too," Matt smiled. Dolly took the order back behind the counter and into the kitchen. Matt looked around and examined the other patrons without staring. The dryads from the day before were back, along with a pair of slender, androgynous youths with long, pointed ears. There was a small group of college-aged magi using wands to put syrup onto their pancakes and lift bacon to each other's mouths. A satyr with furry legs and a goat face put on a hat and his form shimmered into a short, balding man that looked like he could have been an accountant. The accountant put on a protective face mask and strode confidently out the door.

"Most folks in the Fold don't leave the house without a glamour these days," Dolly said, putting Matt's breakfast on the counter. "You're lucky you look so human."

"I try not to forget it," Matt said, picking up his fork and knife.

"You should try the muffin first."

Curious, Matt picked up the muffin and peeled off a part of the top, crisp and brown with a big, juicy blueberry peeking out. Dolly watched him with a smile and he put the whole morsel in his mouth.

"It's good," Matt nodded. "It's sweet, but the blueberry flavor is still there."

"What about the texture?" Mira asked, popping out from behind the counter. Matt coughed a little, surprised that she'd snuck up behind

Dolly and hidden when Matt wasn't looking. "It's too dry, isn't it? Does it feel too much like bran? I worry it's too bran-y."

"Mira," Dolly put a hand on her shoulder, "people have been asking about them all morning. They taste good."

"I've only ever made muffins a couple times," Mira said. "And even then, they were just kinda whipped together in what I could cook by the fire. You're sure they're not too dry?"

"Honestly, it tastes great," Matt said, taking a sip of water. "And hey, now I'm very awake."

"There, you got to see him try it," Dolly said, waving Mira off. "Now, get back to the kitchen and tend the next batch! We can't make them fast enough!"

Mira beamed and scampered back to the kitchen, wiping her hands on her apron.

"Glad that she's settling in well," Matt said.

"She's been a great help. Eager, happy to work. Even Daryl doesn't mind her in the kitchen, which is a rare treat indeed!"

Dolly jerked a thumb toward the kitchen and Matt could see Mira working at a sink full of dishes through the order window. Behind her was a dwarf plodding between a steaming griddle and three large pots. Matt guessed the dwarf was only about four feet tall but broader in the shoulders than any man Matt had ever seen, with a braided beard tucked into a hairnet. His left arm was an appendage of clockwork and brass, gears turning visibly at the bulky shoulder as the dwarf flipped pancakes on the griddle. Daryl stomped around the kitchen, slapping

66

his spatula against the flat top each time he finished flipping or stirring something.

"He's not the easiest to get along with," Dolly continued, "but he cooks like a master. As long as he and Mira don't fight? She can stay as long as she likes."

"That means a lot, I'm sure," Matt smiled. "It's good of you to give her a place to stay."

"Fold looks after our own. Even if she's never lived up top before? She's one of us."

Dolly clopped off to attend to a few of the other tables. Matt picked at his breakfast, finishing the muffin before moving on to anything else on the plate. He took a paper napkin and wrote down some observations about the diner, talking with Dolly when she would walk by. Matt knew he wouldn't be able to ask questions like he wanted, so he had to watch and observe to get information until he could talk with Mira.

As the breakfast rush slowly died down, Mira was released from her work in the kitchen. She eagerly took a place next to Matt at the counter and ate the pancakes and bacon that Dolly put in front of her. The waitress also included one of Mira's muffins on the plate.

"It's only fair you get to enjoy one," Dolly said. "You earned that and more."

Mira smiled and took a bite of the muffin. She chewed it critically, considering the taste, and grinned. "These came out pretty good!"

"You should make them every morning," Matt suggested. "The Mira Muffins!"

"I want to try something different tomorrow," Mira said. "Or maybe cornbread? I found a recipe for croissants, but Daryl doesn't want me doing anything like that until I've had some more practice."

"Well," Dolly smiled. "If these are your first attempt with a real oven? You'll be slinging croissants before you know it!"

The bell over the door rang and Matt turned to see LaBelle entering the diner in the same suit as yesterday. He took off his hat and walked over to sit next to Mira on the corner of the counter. "Hope these kids aren't giving you any grief, Dolly."

"No more trouble than you give me," Dolly laughed, coming over with a plate of steak and eggs for the detective. "In fact, she's done more for me and Daryl this morning than you have in the whole time I've known you."

"Besides my frequent patronage? I also seem to recall a rescue mission for your sister and helping you set this place up."

"And that's why your tab is monthly," Dolly said.

"Do you mind if I borrow Mira and Matt?"

"We can wrap up the morning without her, but I want her back for the after-lunch dishes."

"This will only take a minute," LaBelle said, turning back to Mira. "How are you doing today?"

"Feels good to be here," Mira said, smiling. "I like the Fold so far."

"Good," LaBelle nodded. "I just wanted to let you know I'm going to talk to your clan today—and before you tell me not to, I'm just doing some fact-checking. I want to ask them what they know about your mother. Out of respect, I have to speak with your roslah and maybe the tuckra, if she's available."

"Tuckra?" Matt piped in.

"It's kind of like a historian for the clan?" Mira explained. "Written history isn't our forte, but tuckras keep long oral histories memorized. They're our story keepers and the closest thing we have to law after ritual combat. Mayza, our tuckra, would probably know more about my father than our roslah. My mother was her steward and I helped from time to time."

"Mayza is an old friend of mine," LaBelle said. "I've been meaning to visit, so this is a good reason. I'll save most of my questions for her, but I have to talk with Dural as a sign of respect. I can't just go poking around clan affairs without his permission. If he doesn't ask about you, I won't say anything. But I won't lie for you."

Mira nodded sadly and picked at her breakfast. LaBelle took a sip of black coffee and ate some eggs before digging into his steak.

"What are we supposed to do while you're doing that?" Matt asked. "Are we just supposed to sit here and do nothing?"

"I still don't know why you're here, frankly," LaBelle said. "But if I can't keep you away from this, I can keep you from walking into the Under without being prepared for it. Go home, Matt. Go back to work. Do yourself a favor and stay out of this."

"I can't go back to the grocery store and help Mira at the same time."

"Then you see the point I'm trying to make," LaBelle said, cutting off a piece of steak. "Look, stay or go. But don't be surprised when you get in over your head. If you refuse to leave? Feel free to keep Mira company and out of trouble, but I'm not gonna give you busy work just to keep you from annoying me."

"No, I want to help. If the three of us work together, we can find Mira's dad three times as fast. I might not be as literate in the Under as you two, but I know the Above pretty well. You don't seem like you're in a position to be picky about who your friends are."

"I have plenty of friends," LaBelle said. "I can do this on my own. And I wouldn't get too attached to Mira. I can't make any promises she'll be around if I don't find anything."

"So if you can't find anything, you'll just give up?"

"Matt," Mira said, gently, "trolls don't like losing members of their clan. Negotiations of marriages between clans can last days to ensure no one feels like they're losing a clan member. If I can't find my dad, the value I bring to the clan still has worth that needs to be compensated if I want to go."

"What do you mean?"

"With each extra mouth, comes two extra hands," Mira recited. "Even if most of my clan hates me and no one wants to be my parent, they still want me for the value of work I provide for them. That means I can't just walk away. Without parents, I would belong to the clan collectively."

"So you're their property?"

"No, I'm part of their productivity. Clans don't war for territory anymore, so they measure greatness by what they can make. If my clan produces more food and another clan asks for it, that clan has to hold us in higher esteem. Having more than what's needed is a mark of honor. So, more trolls to do labor means more esteem for the clan. The more esteem for a clan, the more power they hold among other clans."

"You can't leave when members of your clan won't help you survive?"

"They see it as me earning my seat at the clan fire. I snuck away this time, but if I can't find a claim to parentage—within the clan or outside of it—I'll have to earn my way into the clan for food, shelter… everything. If I want to leave, I'll need to offer them something of equal value or get adopted to a new family through blood ties. If we can't find my dad, the only way I can get adopted is through ritual combat. No one would risk that for a half-troll."

"Not as easy as we'd like it to be, huh?" LaBelle asked, eating the last piece of his steak. "By troll law, Mira isn't allowed to have possessions until she's eighteen. And the clan won't let her leave if she can't pay her way out. Unless someone is willing to take the responsibility of raising her."

"Which is why she needs to find her dad," Matt nodded. "This isn't just about you finding him, it's about escaping the clan."

"There might be another way," Mira explained, "but this is the only surefire way. Trolls have to respect parentage above productivity. A child belongs to their family first and community second."

LaBelle set his utensils down and picked up his coffee cup. "If her father can accept the role of her parent—even for a couple of years? Mira won't be in the clan's debt anymore. Understand?"

"That's cruel."

"Welcome to the Under," LaBelle took a final sip of his coffee and wiped his mouth. "I'm going to go talk to the clan. If you want to help? Be Mira's friend. We'll figure out the rest when it comes to it. I can't make any promises except that I'll get Mira where she belongs: Above or Under."

###

After she finished the breakfast dishes, Dolly said that Mira could take the afternoon off. She'd need to come back in the early evening to help with the dinner rush, but Dolly didn't want Mira to exhaust herself in the Above. Matt followed Mira to her lodgings upstairs, a small bedroom with a dresser of drawers and a bed. Mira's yellow raincoat was hanging off the end of the footboard and she hung her new work apron on one of the drawer knobs.

"Pretty barebones," Matt said, noting the blank walls.

"I didn't come up with a lot," Mira shrugged, sitting on her bed. "It's just until LaBelle can find my dad. Then I can focus on making a space into a home"

"Well, then let's make the Above feel more like home while you're here."

"What do you mean?"

"If there's a chance you might have to go back to the Underfolk, maybe we should do something that you can't do in the Under."

"You're serious?"

"I'm taking my new role as best friend very seriously," Matt insisted. "Come on, what's something you want to do here that you can't do in the Under?"

"A lot of it would require a glamour," Mira shrugged. "Like ride an elevator or go to a hot dog cart."

"I appreciate the need for simple things."

"Yeah, but—" Mira pointed to her tusks, poking out of her protruding jaw. "It's not easy to hide this."

"Well, we can't do everything on your list, but maybe we can do one thing. Something outside! With quarantine, a lot of stuff is closed, but we could go to the park? No hot dog carts, but I bet you don't get a lot of trees underground."

Mira folded her hands together and took a deep breath. There were so many things that she wanted to see in the Above. With Matt, she felt like she could actually explore her new world and not worry about the Oak Hand as much. She thought about the stories of her mother's explorations in the Above, trying to determine if anything would be available to a half-troll with very little money in a plagued world. As much as Mira wanted to explore, however, she felt bad goofing around while LaBelle was working as hard as he was to find her father. LaBelle wouldn't give them anything to do, but they could help without getting in the way of his investigation. It was like the kitchen: Mira could do dishes without getting in the way of Daryl's griddle. Matt and Mira just had to find where the dishes were in this investigation.

After thinking a minute, she made a decision. "Could we go to North Point?"

"The pier? Sure! If that's where you wanna go. Why North Point?"

"Because that's where the mermaids are."

<u>Chapter 7</u>

LaBelle strolled easily down the street and into the small bookshop. With the quarantine, LaBelle was comfortable using one of the more common Under Doors. Normally, he'd travel to one of the more remote doors or use a teleporting spell, but it made more sense to take one of the street entrances close to Dolly's. If LaBelle remembered right, the bookshop put him squarely over the Fae Quarter and he felt more welcome in the shelves of literature than in other parts of the Under.

"Sorry, sir," an old man urged, tottering up to the front entrance. His gray hair thinned to nothing at the top of his head, mirrored by a wispy beard beneath the large glasses that made his eyes look huge on his face. "We're only doing pickup orders for the time being."

"I'm searching for a particular book," LaBelle walked over, grinning. "It's called *The Four Trials of Andailia*."

A flash of recognition passed over the old man's face and he smiled. "I'm afraid we're all out. Can I interest you in a copy of *The Seven Tales of the Seven Wives*?"

"You might be able to convince me to leave with a copy of *Eight Nights of Selvier*," LaBelle grinned. The book titles were all nonsense, of course, but the call and response combination told the bookseller that LaBelle was of the Under and the other half told LaBelle that the old man knew who he was.

The bookseller took off his large glasses with a grin and his face shimmered to reveal a single, brown eye that took up most of the man's forehead as the glamour faded away. His gray beard puffed out a bit more and the cyclops straightened from his hunched crouch until his head nearly scraped the ceiling. The cyclops crouched in his bookshop and smiled once his glamour was completely gone. "Welcome back, Mr. LaBelle."

"Always a pleasure, Lanvia," LaBelle beamed up at him. The old cyclops laughed and engulfed LaBelle in a big hug that lifted the detective off the ground. LaBelle patted the old man on the back and was carefully put back on his feet.

"It's good to see you, my old friend! I haven't had a chance to properly stand since the pandemic started, so I'm glad to be in good company. What do you need? I have a rare spell book from France that might tickle your fancy."

"I'm actually just looking to use the Under Door."

"Of course!" The cyclops smiled and gestured towards the shelves. "It's in the back between History and World Travel."

"Thanks, Lanvia," LaBelle grinned and patted the cyclops's shoulder. As the cyclops went back to organizing shelves, LaBelle strode through the corridors of musty, old books. Considering all the entrances to the Under, LaBelle thought there was no door better than this bookshop. Lanvia would no doubt bring the best stories to the Fae Queen and stand sentinel over the doorway as a physical and literary gatekeeper to the Under. LaBelle knew the passwords to every Under Door in the city and beyond. As rarely as he used the public entrances, the bookstore was his favorite for the comfortable smell of old paper and glue that had followed him through the centuries. Nostalgia was a weakness, but he welcomed the chance to feel calm.

Deep in the shelves, LaBelle traced his hand over the spines of history. A lot of what Lanvia kept was from the last two thousand years, some of LaBelle's freshest memories preserved in already decaying tomes. He could remember throwing glass bottles in the French Revolution and in the same breath he could flashback to looking up in the Sistine Chapel for the first time. While he'd never been nobility, LaBelle could recall the kingdoms that he had graced with his presence: all the Henrys, all the Richards, and many of the French aristocrats right up until the last Louis. LaBelle would come and go, but he always went to pay his respects to heads of state of whatever country he called home at the time. He wandered through a shelf of biographies and quickly recalled as much as he could about each name.

"Nice person," LaBelle mused to himself, "terrible singer…racist drunk…too soft-spoken for politics…not half as talented as his ego made you think…ah, she was a sweetheart."

Books were a constant for LaBelle. After traversing the ocean so many times, LaBelle felt that each trip brought a different, new technology. However, he was never tempted to put pen to paper and attempt to write his life story. He would occasionally write notes for cases but never struggled to recall his personal history enough to write anything down. His memory was a steel trap for joy and misery.

As the world travel section approached, LaBelle turned between the shelves and walked right up to the wall. There was a small, irregular carpet that covered the floor and LaBelle bent over, unconsciously covering the action by retying his shoe. He pulled the carpet up and revealed a door like a safe with a gold-colored handle and a spinning knob without numbers. LaBelle twisted in the correct combination by listening to the clicks of the dial, the same combination that granted him entry into the store. The lock clicked and LaBelle twisted the handle up to throw the hatch open, revealing a ladder that went down into a concrete tunnel. When he was sure no one had crept up behind him, LaBelle climbed in and closed the hatch behind him.

Pulling out his thin wand, LaBelle made the tip glow so he could see more than a few inches ahead and walked down the concrete passage. The tunnels were deathly quiet, but LaBelle knew there was nothing more menacing in the pipes than him. He followed the pathway for a while, dropping down another two levels and following a slow decline that brought him down past even the deepest levels of human construction. A dull, orange glow caught his attention while the sound of music and laughter echoed through the tunnels. LaBelle extinguished his wand and slid it back into his holster as he strode into Fae Town.

'Fae Town' wasn't a singular place like Hedgefield. Fae Town was always at the core of any Undercity. Fae folk had lived in places before humans named them, so they didn't need to specify their towns as exactly as humans or magi. Wherever fae congregated and felt at home was Fae Town and under the rule of the Fae Queen.

The Fae Town under Hedgefield was a place of near-constant chaos and celebration. Fae folk—from the smallest fairy to the grandest centaur—were wearing garlands of flowers, striking drums, and sharing goblets of fae wine. Magic here was chaotic, an explosive force of nature that wasn't controlled or contained. Fae Town was one of the few places where magic was visibly bouncing from wall to wall, spiraling like out-of-control firecrackers or drunken fireflies. The music of deep horns and drums that vibrated in LaBelle's chest was overwhelming and cacophonous, rattling LaBelle's bones and thumping in time with his heart. Naiads skipped across the surface of a clear pond, splashing water at one another. Fairies chased each other overhead like a long string of lights twinkling. Centaurs and satyrs danced together, sharing goblets of sweet-smelling fae wine and feeding each other fresh fruit conjured from vines creeping down the edges of the buildings. Ramshackle houses stood beside ornate towers that spiraled up towards a giant, orange-gold crystal that served as a replacement sun for the hidden world.

"LaBelle!"

Turning to the deep, jovial voice, LaBelle grinned. A satyr with a ratty top hat splashed through the fountain, laughing. The hat sported two gaping holes from the satyr's large, curling horns and he wore a long coat with sprigs of herbs and flowers growing out of sewn-on pockets. The satyr cheered and ran over to hug LaBelle. The detective laughed and clasped his arms around the satyr.

"Viscount Valont," LaBelle smiled and bowed slightly. "What's the call for celebration?"

"Eh, someone's birthday, I suppose?" The satyr shrugged absently. "I can't tell anymore, but it's very likely many birthdays at once. Come! Drink with us!"

"I wish I could, my friend," LaBelle shook his head. "I'm here on business, I'm afraid."

"Business, business, business!" Viscount Valont shook his head. "You're older than anyone, but how can you work so much and be in such good health?"

"I like to keep busy," LaBelle laughed. "Tell you what: there's bound to be someone's birthday on Monday, yes? I'll swing by for a cup of fae wine first thing after the weekend."

"Ah!" Viscount Valont gave LaBelle a few playful jabs to the shoulder. "You're a man of good humor after all! The Fae Queen will bring you into our ranks one day!"

"If she can't, it's not for lack of trying," LaBelle smiled. He carefully wove through a few congregations of fae folk, playfully running with a few fae children and kicking the ball back into their game. The sweet smells of fairy food wafted through the air, savory and sweet enough to make a human's stomach revolt with hunger. The Above was in disarray and struggling, but the fae folk were thriving in this chaotic tide.

LaBelle chuckled as he left Fae Town. Fae Town was the epicenter of the Underfolk, where magic was wild and free before being taken and refined by the magi. LaBelle always thought of their use of magic like humans controlling water. The fae let magic do as it would, drifting around until fae folk would reach out for threads of magic to suit their needs. Magi stored and used the magic for their own whims, like humans irrigating the rain and rivers. The Beasts, now the furthest from magic, wanted nothing to do with spell casting and relied on their strength to survive. LaBelle didn't notice a major difference between the three factions otherwise. Still, the social and physical structures of the Under Cities made sure all the inhabitants got the magic they wanted and everyone was kept safe.

Brodal, under Hedgefield, was considered the capital of all the magi Under Cities for the presence of the Victory Tower. The obelisk was improbably large for an underground world and made of dark obsidian bricks that seemed to constantly be shifting like water with a bead of gold light emanating from the apex. Waves of magic would get caught in the spire's magical field like a wind turbine that magi could refine and reshape later with runic rings. LaBelle nodded calmly to the three elves stationed at the city entrance, armored in traditional garb with bronze plate armor and short swords. The elves nodded back, satisfied that this traveler meant no ill will.

The cities of the magi looked like older human cities, with cobblestone streets and buildings made of brick or some other stone. Compared to Fae Town, there was a careful order. Cities were separated into districts for shopping, living, crafts, and administration. LaBelle had come in through the shopping district, an entrance surrounded by collapsable merchant stands that were eager to get business from people coming in from Fae Town. LaBelle had seen the businesses shift and change with the times as often as the Above.

"Hey, you!" An elf called to LaBelle as he walked into the city. "You look like a man of taste! How would you like an enchanted belt? There's magic woven into each stitch for protection and—"

"Don't listen to that soft-handed seamstress!" A dwarf shouted from a stand across from the elf. "You want protection? I have fireproof armor! I did the rune work myself…with real rubies!"

"The safest path is to avoid danger!" A witch leaned out of her stall. "Good luck charms and safety potions! You'll never walk into hazards unprepared again. The first one's free!"

With a smile, LaBelle waved the various merchants off. The sellers redoubled their efforts to catch his attention with other promises of protection, love, and power. A few passing magi civilians in the street would stop and pick through their wares, but LaBelle didn't have time to shop around today. He could make most of the items offered on his own, but he did admire their skill.

"LaBelle!" Aili walked down the street, still barefoot and in her long, flowing dress that she'd worn in the Council yesterday. She approached LaBelle briskly with a bright smile, even though a few of the shopkeepers and customers shied away at the mention of his name. They bowed their heads and greeted Aili with respect, but LaBelle inspired quiet fear in the bustling bazaar. "I didn't know you were coming to our little corner of the Under."

"Things have been very last minute recently," LaBelle explained, "but you seemed to find me by a happy accident. I'd have called ahead if I had time to chat, but I'm on my way to the Outerlands."

"There's time for us to talk then." Aili walked at LaBelle's left with her hands behind her back.

"I can't discuss my case."

"Oh, I wouldn't dream of asking. Tell me how things are in the Above?"

"Disease, anger, fear…it's a hard time for humans."

"And the Underfolk of the Fold?"

"It's a mix. They've always taken solace in their own company. The magi are doing well, as far as I can tell, but my only metric is the folk who go to Dolly's. Before the pandemic up Above, I spoke to Lo'rei of the Yellowstone Woods. She's comfortably defending her ancestral lands with the Spearfolk."

"I'll be sure to pass her well-being along to her father."

"I helped relocate another vampire last week. The Oak Hand raided a nest and killed the rest of their congress. I got confirmation that they made it to the new group. A pair of werewolves needed to find new hunting grounds in California, so I worked out an agreement with the Redwood Bowmen. One hunt a month in exchange for getting jobs with the park service to dissuade curious humans from the Bowmen village."

"It's a shame you had no interest in politics," Aili said. "You would have made a hell of a councilor if you ever settled on a faction."

"I prefer to think of myself as an independent," LaBelle said. "Though some would call me a spy."

"You're too old to care what others think. Can you tell me anything of the Outerlands?"

"Purely a fact-finding mission, I assure you."

"The half-troll."

"I can't confirm that."

"You don't have to," Aili said. "I hope you're successful."

As they walked further, LaBelle told Aili what he could about the Above and she told him of the most recent research at the Victory Tower. LaBelle made a few suggestions from what he knew of previous attempts but mostly listened to Aili's magical theories. She was wise beyond her years and LaBelle thought she would be more talented than any sorceress he'd ever met. Time passed quickly and LaBelle was on the outskirts of Brodal somewhere in a conversation about wand making. LaBelle only stopped when he noticed Aili was no longer by his side, frozen in place by fear of what lay beyond her city limits.

"And once more," Aili said, "you go where I dare not follow."

"Until we meet again, my dear," LaBelle smiled and shook her hand. "Perhaps I'll see you at Dolly's one of these days."

"When that time comes, I'll find you, old friend."

Aili left, wrapping her arms around herself as if fighting a chill. LaBelle took a deep breath and crossed the barrier out of Brodal. A monstrous, black animal the size of a horse was chained by the road that led into the sparse Outerlands. As LaBelle approached, the Black Dog rose with a harsh snarl, red eyes blazing against the coal-black fur. The hound growled and snapped at him as he passed by, but LaBelle knew showing fear would only make it stronger. Running would make it want to chase. Flinching could make it bolder. The Outerlands had as many rules as Brodal, but their rules were learned by experience rather than expressed in words.

The light of the crystal over Fae Town didn't extend this far and LaBelle felt like he was always just entering the mouth of a cave, leading to an overcast mood that followed LaBelle into the dark. There were few beasts awake during the day, but he saw goblins skittering in the dark to scrounge for food and supplies. A lone minotaur lumbered by and might have threatened LaBelle with the battle-ax he dragged in the dirt behind him. However, the bovine humanoid thought better and let the detective pass by without issue. Harpies fought over something dying in the distance and LaBelle pitied the poor thing for a moment. This was the order of the Outerlands.

LaBelle walked further in the perpetual twilight until he took his first steps into the troll camps. He walked carefully, keeping to no specific clan territory's invisible lines. Trolls grunted and growled on either side of him, but LaBelle ignored them. From what he knew of trolls, it was best to not even risk glancing to ensure it wouldn't be mistaken for a challenge. He kept moving until he reached the outer limits of the Copper Tooth Clan.

The dwellings of trolls in the past were caves, wooden frames with leafy roofs, or even the occasional bridge to protect them from the harsher elements. In the Under, trolls set up their homes beneath blue construction tarps supported by discarded fishing rods or broom handles. They used pieces of abandoned cars to fortify their camp and flipped stolen buses onto their sides to create barricades as a show of force against potential invaders that LaBelle knew would never come. A large fire burned in the middle of the Copper Tooth camp, stretching out the shadows and casting silhouettes of the trolls against their tarp village.

"Blanc LaBelle," a deep voice rumbled from behind. LaBelle turned and saw Roslah Dural Copper Tooth glaring down at him from an imposing seven feet tall with broad shoulders and muscles that made him a little hunched. The gray, muddled hide of the head troll was flecked with growths that looked like stone and fungus. His right forearm had been broken purposefully to create a stone shield or heavy club with jagged calcium deposits breaking through the skin. He was wearing a rough shirt and pants made from bed sheets, as well as a royal-looking fur cloak from a black bear. The cloak could have easily been a family relic, but LaBelle wouldn't doubt that Dural Copper Tooth could kill even the biggest black bear he could find. The massive troll only looked down on LaBelle physically. LaBelle's reputation was too well known for him to be truly looked down upon.

"I believe," Dural grumbled, "you have something that belongs to me."

<u>Chapter 8</u>

"Mermaids?"

"Yup."

"At North Point?"

"Yup!"

"I've been there dozens of times," Matt said. "Why haven't I seen any before?"

"Maybe you didn't know how to look," Mira shrugged. Matt stewed a little, trying to process another piece of big news. After getting permission from Dolly to go adventuring, Mira changed into her yellow raincoat and put her mask on over her nose and mouth. Dolly warned her to be careful and to come back by four o'clock to help with the dinner crowd. Mira eagerly drove off with Matt, taking in all the details of the city as they rode to North Point Beach. Matt had been barraging her with questions since they left the diner. Mira was more animated than the day before, excited to be Matt's guide out in the world for a change.

"I think it wouldn't be hard to spot a mermaid on the beach," Matt said. "What kid doesn't keep their eyes on the ocean looking for something exciting?"

"Fae folk have been slipping in and out of the Under for decades. If humans can see them, it's only because they want to be found."

"But you can find them?"

"It's kind of a mutual respect."

"Are you a fae folk?"

"No, I'm a beast."

"You shouldn't say that about yourself."

"No, it's not like that," Mira said. "It's just what we call our faction. All Underfolk live underground, but we all have different relationships with humans that split us into factions."

"Such as?"

"The short answer? The fae folk want to bring humans down with us, the magi want the Underfolk to stay in the Under, and the beasts will usually kill humans on sight."

"Except for your mom?"

"There's always exceptions. My mom didn't hate humans and fae folk like Dolly are willing to come up and live in the Above. I even know of a few magi who are quite content to stay in the Under… vampires mostly."

"So, what makes Dolly a fae and not a magi? Or trolls beasts and not fae?"

"Honestly? Those distinctions were made long before even Mayza was born. It has something to do with magic, but beasts aren't really educated on something we don't use."

"And because you're all Underfolk, mermaids will trust you?"

"Like I said, it's an understanding. If we can find a mermaid, they'll know I won't put them in danger and I know I can trust them to help me."

"Sounds like a better arrangement than the Above. I barely trust my coworkers not to eat my lunch."

Mira laughed and looked out the window. Matt turned down towards the pier and parked his car in the empty beach parking lot. As Mira climbed out, she was taken by the sensations of the ocean surrounding her. Seagulls were flying overhead, calling to one another and occasionally resting on the shore to pick through a discarded hot dog before flying away from the oncoming waves. The breeze over the water carried the taste of salt and the smell of fish.

The only other people at the public beach were an older man painting the seascape and a young couple throwing a ball across the sands for their massive gray dog. The hound perked up and ran over to the newcomers on the beach. Mira shied away behind Matt when the dog galloped up to them, but Matt just smiled and took the ball from the dog's fuzzy jaws.

"It's okay," Matt said. "He's just playful." Matt handed the ball over to Mira. The dog looked up at her, licking his lips and wagging his tail eagerly. The couple at the end of the beach waved their arms at them. Mira took the ball and threw it, sending the dog running down the sand after it. Mira laughed as the dog grabbed the ball out of the air and ran back to his owners.

"I've never seen a dog before," Mira breathed. "I mean, I knew they existed, but I've never met one!"

"Now you know why I'm so nervous about the mermaids?" Matt smiled.

Mira laughed a little and tugged Matt's arm. "Come on," Mira said. "We can go under the pier and call the mermaids there."

Matt nodded and followed Mira along the beach. They walked over some rocks, carefully placing their steps and relying on one another for balance. Mira gripped Matt's shoulder as they walked over the stones and hopped down into the sand, splashing in the middle tide and walking around the beams that held the pier above them. The water was frigid as it splashed on Mira's ankles and she hopped from rock to rock to avoid stepping in the ocean.

"Here should work," Mira said, taking a few steps towards the tide. She leaned down and splashed the surface of the water with a flat hand. "Hello?" she called. "If anyone is here, I'd like to see you."

"I don't think that's gonna—"

"My name is Mira," she said, pulling her mask off. "I'm of the Copper Tooth Clan. Please, I could use a familiar face today."

Mira waited for a moment, scanning the surface of the water. She kept still, occasionally splashing the tide as it came close to her. A dark, smooth dome broke the surface, but it retreated into the ocean beyond her reach.

"There!" Mira pointed. "Did you see?"

"It might just be a seal," Matt reasoned.

"Oh, have a little imagination!" Mira whispered, before raising her voice. "You can come out. Matt's probably one of the nicest people I've met in the Above. You can come closer, you have my word."

There was another moment of quiet and the shape returned to the surface. It hesitated longer this time before moving closer to the shore. Mira saw the form slither behind another tree trunk-like support of the pier and a pair of hands with green scales gripped the beam.

"Hello," Mira smiled. "What's your name?"

The hands slipped back into the water and the shape moved closer. Mira could see the smooth, slick hair of a human head with patches of scales under their eyes and around their chin. The woman's face smiled and she floated on the water to keep her head visible. The mermaid had long, black hair that pooled around her and light brown skin. She smiled and showed a mouthful of straight, white teeth that came to slight points. Mira had seen mermaids before, but they rarely smiled after swimming around in the sewers.

"My name is Tika," the mermaid smiled. "I didn't think I'd find any beasts so far in the Above."

The mermaid crawled through the sea foam and dragged her slim form up the shoreline using a wave for momentum. Pulling herself forward by her forearms, Tika revealed splashes of green scales on her shoulders, back, stomach, and chest, blending her skin in with the green, fanned tail that splashed in the water behind her. She scrutinized Mira, arching her back to get a good look at her. "You don't look like any troll I've seen before."

"Have you met a lot of trolls?"

"A handful." Tika rolled onto her back and lounged in the sand. "Most of them are bigger and rougher than you."

"I'm only half-troll," Mira said. "My father was human."

"And this one," Tika rolled onto her stomach again and grinned passed Mira. "Your 'Matt'? Is he your half-brother?"

"Matt's…" Mira looked over at Matt and smiled. "Matt's my friend; probably my best friend."

"Then I welcome you, Matt," Tika splashed a little in the water and propped up on her elbows. "It is not often that I get company. The sea creatures don't offer as many cultured conversations."

"Is it true that mermaids can tell prophecies?" Mira blurted out. "You're fae, right?"

"Not all fae folk are capable of telling fortunes," Tika said. "Just as all fae are not capable of granting wishes."

"But no fae can lie," Mira said. "They can twist the truth or hide it, but they can't deny the truth."

Tika smiled and giggled into the water. "How clever…you must know the fae folk well."

"So, can you see the future?"

"The future? No," Tika frowned. "That is a privilege reserved for a few select fae. Too many options that only a handful who can look through the Veil can truly comprehend and fewer can see them all while keeping their wits."

"What about the past?" Mira asked. "Sometimes fortune isn't about what will happen."

"Ah, the past," Tike grinned. "I can see the pasts of others."

"Can you look into my past for me?"

"Mira—" Matt started.

"I just wanna see if she can tell me anything."

"What about LaBelle?" Matt asked.

"If my clan doesn't help, we might be able to get something useful from Tika," Mira explained before turning back to the mermaid. "I need to know about my father. Can you look into my past and tell me who he is?"

"I can try," Tika nodded. She scooted up the sand and sat, curling her tail underneath her. The mermaid held Mira's palms and looked deep into the half-troll's eyes. "Focus on the question you want to know. What is the truth you really want to know? You don't need the perfect words, just focus."

Mira closed her eyes and swallowed. "I want to know anything you can tell me about my father."

Tika closed her eyes and let out a deep breath. Matt looked around them, making sure they were still being left alone. The sounds of seagulls and surf drowned out the conversation to any eavesdroppers, but Matt figured the pair would want to know if a human was coming.

"I see…" Tika said, keeping her eyes gently closed, "a troll woman. She's smaller and hiding among humans with a mask."

"My mother."

"Yes," Tika nodded. "I can see her now."

"What about my father?"

"There are so many humans," Tika said. "She's moving so easily through the crowd and no one is screaming. They can't see her—no, they can! They just don't see what she is. Everyone is wearing a mask."

"Like a party?" Matt asked, excited. "Is she at a Halloween party?"

"I don't know," Tika shook her head. "She's the only troll there."

"What about my father? Do you see a man there?"

"I—I don't see anything yet. Wait, I can see—no, I can't. He's hidden."

"Hidden?" Mira asked, desperate. "What do you mean?"

"It's like…bright light is all around him," Tika said, closing her eyes tighter and turning away like she was being blinded. "It's like he swallowed the sun and it's shining out of every pore of his body."

"What can you see?" Mira asked, gripping Tika's hands tighter. "Tell me anything you can see!"

"They're talking, but I can't hear the words."

"What's he wearing?" Mira pleaded.

"He's a blur of light and gray."

"Gray?" Mira pressed.

"Yes! He's wearing a gray suit, but I can't see his face. It's—gah!" Tika squeezed her eyes tighter, trying to block out the light. Her shoulders were tight and Mira felt Tika's grip squeeze as she tried to stay in the vision. The mermaid exhaled, opened her eyes, and blinked a few times with a deep sigh. "I lost it. I'm sorry."

"Can you look again?"

"Mira," Tika sighed, exhausted. "It was hard enough to look back the first time, I doubt I could do it again with different results."

"Try!" Mira urged, squeezing her hands tighter.

"Mira," Matt stepped forward.

"You're hurting me!" Tika said, trying to pull away.

"Please!" Mira begged. "You have to try again! There has to be something you can see!"

"Mira, stop!" Matt said, grabbing her shoulders. Mira was startled and released Tika's hands. The mermaid recoiled and jumped away from the others. She frantically pushed off the shore and jumped into the water headfirst, arching her back and sliding under the water. Her tail slipped in last, standing straight up before disappearing quietly underwater.

"Shit, shit, shit!" Mira cried. She crawled forward, soaking her knees in the surf. "Come back! I'm sorry! I didn't mean to hurt you. Please, come back!"

The mermaid didn't resurface and the only movement was the rolling waves crashing against the sand. Mira didn't move for a minute, slowly breathing and watching the water. Shuddering, Mira cried and her tears dropped into the water. Matt took a few steps forward and gently held her shoulder. She wiped her eyes with the back of her hand, leaving a streak of salt water across her face.

"I'm sorry," Mira shook her head. "This was stupid."

"It's not stupid," Matt assured her. "I just wish you'd told me this was the whole plan."

"It was a dumb idea," Mira said. "I'm so stupid."

"Hey," Matt gripped Mira's shoulder and she looked up at him. He took out a tissue from his backpack and handed it to Mira. "You're not stupid, okay? You wanted to get information and you were proactive about it. I just wish you'd told me about the mermaid prophecy."

"I didn't think you'd believe me." Mira smiled a little and wiped her eyes. She put her mask back on and stuffed the tissue in her pocket. "I just wish we had learned something."

"Maybe we did. Tika said his face was blocked. That can't be common, can it?"

"Not really," Mira shrugged. She scooted back onto a rock to collect herself out of the water. "I've never really gotten a vision from a fae before, but usually people can get some kind of answer in the Veil."

"Then it has to mean something," Matt said.

"The only reasons that someone would be hidden in the Veil is if they were a favored of the Fae Queen, which is pretty rare, or if they're someone so terrifying that they have to be removed from history for everyone's safety: their name, their acts, their appearance."

"Maybe your dad was someone important."

"If that was the case, why wouldn't my mom have told me? My clan would have worn his greatness as our own."

"Well, whoever he was?" Matt said, sitting next to Mira in the sand. "At least you got to show me a mermaid."

"Yeah," Mira sniffled. "I just hope I didn't hurt her."

"Well, maybe today doesn't have to be a total bust. Sure, the mermaid didn't help much, but we still got to go on an adventure, right?"

"Right," Mira sat in the sand and looked out over the waves. "At least the view is nice."

"Hey," Matt nudged Mira's arm with a smile, "let's go see if we can get a better view. I got just the thing."

<u>Chapter 9</u>

"Blanc LaBelle," Dural growled, "where is the halfbreed?"

"I'm not at liberty to say," LaBelle said, calmly, "but rest assured, she's safe."

LaBelle took a few steps further into the troll encampment. The trolls were beginning to gather around their leaders. Some were carrying traditional stone axes passed down through generations and others carried discarded road signs with sharpened edges. A troll woman paused by the conversation with a basket of fish and turtles, her long, white hair braided down to her back. Two troll children hid behind their mother, eager to hear the conversation, but not interested in entering any conflict with the roslah.

"She is our clan," Dural grunted. "She is our right."

"No one is anyone's right," LaBelle said. "Mira is not your property."

"But she is our responsibility!" Another troll stepped forward, puffing out his chest and towering over LaBelle. His left hand was broken so completely that there was no visible flesh within the giant stone knot at the end of his arm. His white hair was shaved into a mohawk and he wore brass rings down the bridge of his nose. It was hard to judge the emotions of trolls, but LaBelle could tell this troll was snarling with disgust and anger as he spoke. "With her mother dead, the burden of parenthood falls to the clan!"

"I don't think I know you," LaBelle said, not looking away from this new troll.

"This is Kenos," Dural said, proudly, "our new kessra for the clan."

"I thought clan champions went out of style ages ago? There haven't been clan disputes like that since before the Under Pact."

"Traditions come back when they are needed," Kenos said, raising his stone fist. "When Dural needs clan law enforced? I am his left hand."

"Well, Kenos," LaBelle began, "Mira is not your responsibility if you aren't willing to take proper care of her."

"Her traitor mother owed us a child!" Kenos snapped. "If she'd had a troll child like she was supposed to, we wouldn't have this problem and her father would be among the clan! Since her mother died, Mira belongs to the clan that raised her."

"Unless," LaBelle corrected, "another parent can be found. Mira believes her father is still alive. By your law, he has the right to accept or deny parentage before she is a clan child. All I'm asking is that you give me time to find her father and let him know about the option."

"And expose all of our kind to—!"

"I have permission from the Council," LaBelle said, raising his voice over Kenos's shouting. "Both to find Mira's father and offer him parentage rights. But, if you like, I'm sure the Great Dragons would be happy to confirm it. We all know how Extoran likes to be bothered by me."

There was a brief moment where Kenos looked ready to swing at LaBelle with his club of a hand. Dural stepped between Kenos and LaBelle, glaring back at the younger troll. LaBelle knew that Dural hadn't become roslah by following his rage. Kessras were bred to fight other trolls, but LaBelle wasn't someone that Dural wanted a war with.

"Very well," the troll leader said. "You have until midnight. Then you will bring the halfbreed back to us."

"Day after tomorrow," LaBelle said. "I'm good, but these things take time."

"Tomorrow night," Dural replied. "Each day she is missing is a day she could work for the clan."

"I'll try," LaBelle sighed. "I'll have her back the following morning at the latest."

"Sundown tomorrow," Dural said, firmly. "With the halfbreed."

"With Mira, yes."

"Then we have an accord," Dural rumbled.

Kenos snarled and stomped away, pushing smaller trolls out of his path. Dural grunted and looked back to LaBelle as the crowd dispersed.

"Don't pay him any mind," Dural said, trying to soothe any animosity towards LaBelle. "He always held affections for Mira's mother, so her betrayal wounded him harder."

"And what do you think of Mira?"

"She's small, runty," Dural said with notable disdain, "but there's work for everyone here. I'd rather she work for us than trounce about the Above like her mother."

"I would like to talk with the tuckra," LaBelle said, relaxing his posture and putting his hands in his pockets. "I think Mayza will have a better sense of where I should focus my investigation."

"Granted," Dural said. "Whatever it takes to get this resolved."

"I appreciate your cooperation," LaBelle said, following Dural further into the camp. "It takes a strong roslah to give his people their choices."

"For Mira, it's the illusion of choice. You and I both know that her father—whoever he is—won't accept her. Humans can only see with their eyes. The sooner we confirm that he won't take her, the sooner the halfbreed will be brought home."

"Perhaps," LaBelle said. "But the law is the law and her father has the right to choose. You will accept if he agrees to take her, just as I will accept if he doesn't."

Dural grumbled something, but LaBelle didn't push him any further. His relationships with the beasts were not perfect, so he tried not to antagonize them. While the Magi Prima and the Fae Queen would offer him protection, the Great Dragons offered reluctant indifference. Extoran, in particular, wouldn't blame the trolls for reacting to LaBelle's rudeness according to their traditions.

"The tuckra is there," Dural said, motioning to a ring of cars with a tarp over the middle and a thin tendril of smoke worming out through a metal smoke stack. "Be sure to pay her the proper respect. Hiding Mira from us is already a slight against the clan. It would be unwise to offend Mayza and dishonor the clan further."

"I mean no offense," LaBelle said, raising his hands. "I thank you for escorting me. I will offer my respects on my way out."

Dural nodded, taking a few steps backward before turning his back on LaBelle. The troll leader stomped back to the main cluster of trolls by the large, central fire. LaBelle turned and pushed back the blue plastic tarp that separated the tuckra's lodge from the outside world.

Tuckra Mayza was old. As the voice of the troll's clan's past, she was a powerful figure in the community. LaBelle knew Mayza had outlived the last three clan roslahs. The clan's leadership positions were often based on strength or force, but Mayza's influence came from the things she remembered. Her memory was a living index of "precedent" that was honored as law. The old troll woman had long, spidery limbs with mushrooms growing on her arms and shoulders dotted with warts and a mossy green rash. The troll elder had stringy, white hair, and her lower lip was studded with rings of copper between her tusks. With bleary eyes, she looked up from a bowl of steaming liquid and grinned as LaBelle came in.

"It is unfair," Mayza said in a slow, raspy whisper, "that I should face the ravages of time and you remain untouched."

"Only in body," LaBelle said, sitting across from her. "In spirit, you are still much younger than I."

Mayza chuckled and set her bowl aside. Her long reach didn't require her to move from where she was sitting to grab an empty bowl. Dipping the bowl into the cauldron, Mayza presented LaBelle with some of her boiling brew.

LaBelle graciously took the bowl and drank from it. The liquid was foul-smelling and burned his lips before he even took the first sip. The troll's tea was bitter and salty, but LaBelle had drunk enough of it over the years to resist the urge to vomit. Though no amount of practice could get him to enjoy the taste.

"Why are you here, LaBelle?" Mayza asked, sipping her tea. "You haven't personally stepped down into the Under since…well, I can't recall."

"Things have not been well in the Above. My skills were more useful there than in the Under."

"And we may never know if that is true or not," Mayza nodded. "Even the wisest fae cannot predict what might have been."

"I want to talk to you about Mira," LaBelle said. "It's about her mother."

"Ahh," Mayza nodded, sadly. "Mira is kind. I was distraught when I learned she had run off in the middle of the night."

"You seem to be the only one who cares about her well-being."

"I am far too old," Mayza grumbled, "to care about something as foolish as breeding. She may not look it, but Mira is as much a part of this clan as I am."

"It would simplify the problem if—"

"I am forbidden from adopting into my bloodline. The tuckras cannot be bound by family, only to the clan. If she were older, I would take her as my apprentice. She's smart enough to do my job, but she's still too young and has to be looked over."

"I'm not arguing that she needs supervision," LaBelle said. "I just wish that she could be adopted by someone who cares about her."

"And you think that's only going to be found here in the clan?"

"I don't know," LaBelle shook his head. "I just wish this could be an open and closed case. She belongs here."

"She belongs where she feels safe," Mayza corrected. "If she feels safest with her father, there's no reason for her to be with the clan."

"Then I suppose I should hurry up and find her father," LaBelle said, taking a sip of tea to sharpen his mind. "What can you tell me about Mira's mother?"

"Kaysar was bold, adventurous. Not the sort of troll to accept 'I don't know' as an answer. She had what our clan called the 'Wandering Sickness.' I'm sure you know the type."

"More common among fae or even magi, but I've known a handful of beasts who fancied themselves to be explorers. I've even met a few trolls, but they're careful not to give out much personal information."

"They go to the Above to gather information, not give it," Mayza said, pointing upwards with a bony finger. "The beasts are prohibited from living in the cities of the Above, but visitors will go and bring back valuable information and supplies."

"Explorers to the new world."

"Feels newer each time I hear about it. But that was the draw for Kaysar. She was too curious to leave the Above unknown. Before she had Mira, she would tell me stories of all her visits. Encounters with bus drivers and dog parks! Such a strange world, so close to our own."

"And when Mira was born?"

"When Kaysar didn't tell us who had gotten her pregnant, the rest of the clan thought she was trying to avoid making the others jealous."

"She never gave any indication as to who the father was?"

"There's no precedent that could force a troll woman to reveal the father of her child," Mayza shook her head. "The child is always inducted into the mother's clan, so what use would it be to know the father? But when Mira was born—"

"It was clear Kaysar wasn't hiding a troll partner."

"Kenos and a handful of others were furious, but Mira was declared part of our clan. Mira and her mother helped me here, keeping an old troll's home livable. I was reluctant, but I think you'll find Mira's kindness can break through the layers of even your heart. The truth of Mira's father died with Kaysar. If Mira didn't know, I don't think anyone will."

"But she must have told you something," LaBelle urged. "A name, something about his face, or how they met. If she told you about buses and dogs, she must have told you stories about this handsome stranger."

"She told me of adventures."

"Love is an adventure for some people."

"Bah!" Mayza waved a hand and smiled. "Same LaBelle, equal parts cynic and romantic."

"Live as long as I have and you'd want to believe in something, too," LaBelle grinned, slyly. His smile faded before he could ask his next question. "How did she die?"

"Calcite disease." Mayza looked down pensively into the brewing pot of tea. "Premature calcification happens sometimes in trolls. It was slow, but Mira stayed with her the whole time."

"There must have been something she told you on her death bed."

"My position doesn't give me the right to pry into people's personal lives," Mayza said. "I remembered Mira's birth because it was so bizarre. The last time there was a mix of human and troll was… over three hundred years ago."

"I'd imagine it's an uncommon occurrence. Did Kaysar use a glamour in the Above?"

"Naturally," Mayza affirmed. "Someone from Brodal gave it to her as a gift. A necklace, I think."

"Do you have it?"

"No," Mayza said. "I believe it is still among Kaysar's things. Dural hasn't distributed her belongings to the clan yet. He won't until the matter with Mira is settled."

"If you could look for it—"

"I'll see if I can send it up to you," Mayza promised. "If it isn't enough to give Mira some safety, perhaps it will bring her comfort."

"I'd appreciate that," LaBelle said. He looked down into his tea and begrudgingly took a sip.

"You seem disappointed," Mayza observed. "That sour face is from more than just bad tea."

"I was just expecting more," LaBelle said. "Maybe not a name, but some clue or a hunch I could follow. But why would Kaysar choose to be with a human? Assault had crossed my mind, but it sounds like she loved this man."

"She did," Mayza nodded. "I think she truly did."

"Now who's the romantic?" LaBelle asked, swirling the contents of his bowl. "Then why hide from him? Why not take Mira to the surface and tell him—"

"Even if Kaysar wanted to tell him," Mayza said, "what would you have them do? Tell the father and have them live in the Above?"

"Stranger things have happened."

"Even if Kaysar used her glamour up there?" Mayza pointed upwards with a shaking finger. "They would never accept her as she was. As much as she loved the Above, she always came back here. She was only meant to bring information from the surface, but she knew she could never live there. Mira was the only part of the Above that she allowed herself to keep."

LaBelle ran his index finger along the edge of his bowl, contemplating.

"There's something else?" Mayza asked and took a sip from her bowl.

"I hope it was worth it."

"I think," Mayza nodded, "she would do it all again if you gave her the chance. The way she loved Mira was enough to tell me that. Whoever the father was, Kaysar carried that last piece of her love for him in Mira."

LaBelle frowned and took another sip of his tea. It was bitter, but he thought that might have been the taste of disappointment.

<u>Chapter 10</u>

"This place is normally super busy in the summer," Matt said, "but the theme park was shut down because of the virus. They had the whole pier locked off at first, but people now are allowed to at least walk on the dock."

"It's so quiet up here," Mira said. Along the length of the pier, food and game stalls were all closed up. The kayak rentals were all wrapped up with chains and all the rides were taped off with signs warning people to keep off.

"None of the rides or stands are open," Matt said, "but the view is worth it, I promise." The amusement park still smelled of funnel cake and popcorn butter. Seagulls called out as they picked through garbage bins for the last scraps of carnival food from before the wharf closed. The wood groaned a little under their footsteps, but the creaking boards were drowned out by the sound of waves crashing below the deck. Matt led Mira down to the end of the wooden walkway. Normally, the scenic view was flooded with tourists and fishermen, but the pandemic meant that Matt and Mira were completely alone. Together, the teens looked out over the end of the boardwalk at the expansive ocean ahead of them. Rein Island, a small, tree-covered hump in the distance with a pink square to highlight the abandoned hotel, seemed to only exist to give a sense of the vastness of the ocean.

"This is one of my favorite spots in the city." Matt folded his arms on the railing and took a deep breath of the sea breeze. "I'll even come here on weekends during the winter just to smell the sea air."

Mira leaned forward, wide-eyed and excited. "It's huge! I've never seen anything this big in my life! How far does it go?"

"I don't have a number, but you could go all the way past that curve of the horizon and it will still go on well beyond what you can see."

"Wow," Mira folded her arms and leaned over the railing to look down. "Have you seen it?"

"Seen what?"

"The curve of the horizon."

"Once," Matt said, "when I was a kid. My dad's a pilot—mostly commercial flights these days, but he used to do smaller planes for aerial tours when I was younger. Sometimes in the summer, he'd take me up with him on low attendance tours and I got to see all of

Hedgefield from really high up. Once, my mom and I took a flight with him to California and I got to watch takeoff from the cockpit."

"Where's California?"

"About…2,800 miles that way," Matt pointed towards the land. "On the other side of the country. I think you'd like it. Another ocean on that side and sunny beaches."

"Another ocean?" Mira laughed. "I still need to wrap my head around this one! I'm just coming up to the Above for the first time, I can't imagine going anywhere else."

"Well, there's a lot more than just Hedgefield. Hell, I'm still learning that there's a lot more to Hedgefield."

"Where's your dad now?" Mira asked.

"He was flying over to Washington when someone in his flight crew tested positive for Covid. He's quarantined with family in Seattle. They can't let him go home until they're sure he's not gonna get anyone sick. This disease has been really difficult for everyone to live with."

"My mom died of a disease," Mira said. Her face was hard to read through the mask, but her eyes looked a bit sad in a way her voice didn't betray.

"That sucks," Matt said, knowing it was the only truth he could manage.

"Yeah, calcite disease is a nasty one."

"What's—" Matt started but stopped himself. "Sorry, I shouldn't ask."

"It's a troll disease," Mira said, calm and factual. "One of the benefits trolls have is that if we break a bone, it heals fast…like, next day fast. Our bones instantly release calcium quickly to harden up the bone at the break. I broke my leg when I was ten and I was able to walk on it the next day, once they set it right. I know a couple of trolls that break the bones in their hands to pack a meaner punch. One troll I met fractured his skull so many times it was basically a helmet."

"Sounds like a fun guy," Matt grimaced. "What does that have to do with calcite disease?"

"It's not common," Mira said, "but sometimes the calcification process goes wrong. A bone fractures and it doesn't stop calcifying or the process just starts even when there isn't a broken bone. In my mom's case, the calcification got started in her chest and spread until she couldn't breathe."

"Oh my God, that's awful."

Mira wiped her eyes with the back of her hand. "She had enough time to put things in order. That's more than most trolls get. And I was able to stay with her until the end."

"How long ago was this?"

"We set her in the stoneyard less than a week ago."

"A week? Mira, I'm sorry. I had no idea."

"I didn't expect you to," Mira shook her head. "I had a lot of time to stay with her. The calcite didn't take her for almost two weeks and she fought the whole time."

"And she never said who your father was?"

"It didn't feel like the right time to ask," Mira said. "When I was with her, all I could think about was how to ease her pain or make the process easier for her. By the time I realized it was my last chance to ask her anything, she was almost solid stone."

"Completely?"

"That's what happens when a troll dies," Mira said. "First the bones, then our organs, then muscles and skin. Our stoneyard is filled with trolls that have all calcified."

"Wow," Matt said. "I'm sorry."

"She got to die standing. A lot of trolls in the stoneyard are on their backs, but standing is a mark of bravery and honor. She met her death with strength and I got to be with her."

"And then you jumped right into the Above," Matt said. "I wish you had more time to grieve."

"I've grieved as a troll," Mira said. "I'll grieve as a human when I find my father."

Matt nodded and watched Mira for a moment. She was calm on the surface, but her stare looked out past the island as if she could find her peace beyond where the sky and sea seemed to touch. "Do you… want a hug or something?"

"Yeah," Mira nodded. "That'd be nice."

Matt wrapped his right arm over Mira's shoulders and squeezed. Mira put her head on his chest but didn't cry. He felt her exhale unsteadily and her body relaxed under his arm. They watched the water for a while, only the crashing of waves marking time in the silence. Mira shifted a little and turned to look down the length of the pier over Matt's shoulder. She tensed and gripped his hand. "Matt," Mira whispered, "someone is watching us."

Matt glanced over his shoulder and saw a man with a black windbreaker and sunglasses. He was in his early thirties with black hair and a firm scowl. The man looked away quickly, trying to avoid being caught. While Matt didn't see the stranger's face, flashes of the Oak Hand agents surrounding the grocery store came to mind. Whether the man was dangerous or not, Matt didn't want to test it. "Okay," Matt squeezed Mira's shoulder. "We can make it back to my car. If we don't run, he won't chase us. Just go slow, okay?"

Mira nodded and Matt pulled her close. He turned his back on the stranger and walked back towards their parking spot. Matt looked up at one of the closed ice cream stands, the mirrored surface of the flashy sign reflecting the walkway behind him. He could see the outline of the man's legs as he stalked a few paces behind the duo. Matt kept walking slowly, listening to the footsteps on wood as the stranger closed in on them.

Matt sped up a little, using the reflective windows of the food stalls along the pier to watch the progress of their pursuer. He had to fight the urge to break into a full sprint, but his pace quickened when the man behind them was within a few feet. When he saw the car, Matt grabbed Mira's arm and started running. He reached and turned over a trash can, startling a flock of seagulls and giving him and Mira some more breathing room.

"Hey!" The man yelled after them. "Stop!"

"Don't look back!" Matt told Mira. They were sprinting now as the man raced behind them. Mira started running faster than Matt, so he grabbed the keys from his pocket and put them in Mira's hand. "Mira, get to the diner! I'll buy you some time!"

"I'm not going without you!"

"I can keep this guy busy so you can get to the car. It's been a while since I've done any karate, but I can at least—"

"Matt, get down!"

Matt turned around just in time to drop to the wooden floor as Mira heaved a kayak over her head at the Oak Hand agent charging toward them. The fiberglass missile struck their pursuer and pinned him under the kayak with a thud and a grunt. Climbing back to his feet, Matt looked between Mira and the boat she'd thrown down the pier.

"Since when did you have superpowers?" Matt asked, exasperated.

"I'm half-troll. I'm the weakest in my clan, but that counts for something in the Above."

"Remind me never to get on your bad side," Matt said, glancing at the man splayed under the boat. "Come on, we gotta get—"

A black van pulled into the parking lot, blocking Matt and Mira from the car. The side door slid open and Matt counted four men climbing out before Mira grabbed him and pulled him back down the boardwalk.

"This way!" Matt said, tugging Mira's arm and sliding between a churro place and the kayak rental shop. Matt led Mira through the labyrinth of pop-up shops, carefully checking behind each corner as they moved through the food and game kiosks.

Mira picked up a broom and carried it with them. When they approached an opening towards the carnival rides, she stopped Matt and swung up, striking one of the Oak Hand agents under the jaw. Before the first agent hit the ground, Mira threw her broom handle like a spear and knocked another man so hard in the face that his sunglasses broke in half.

Matt led Mira through the rides, ducking and weaving between the coils of the rollercoaster track. The pair jumped the fence into the tilt-o-whirl but stopped as two Oak Hand agents jumped the fence on the other side. Mira pulled Matt towards the Ferris wheel but changed direction when another agent cut them off. The teens jumped the fence and ran through the carousel, swerving between the plastic animals. Mira was at the fence when Matt felt a big hand grab his shoulder and rip him off his feet.

"Matt!" Mira yelled, moving back towards the fight.

"Mira, run!" Matt shouted, struggling against the man who held him by the arms. Matt kicked his feet, but the agent squeezed tightly around Matt's arms to keep him in place.

"Don't move!" A man ran into the carousel area with the two men Mira had fought off with the broomstick. The leader was much older than the other agents, with a concrete-gray buzzcut and a square head.

He was wearing a button-up shirt and jeans under his windbreaker, but the gun on his waist drew Matt's attention first. He wasn't wearing a mask and looked at Mira with disgust. The other Oak Hand agents surrounded them, cutting off Mira's escape. "Nowhere left to run. Give up."

"Let him go!" Mira yelled, balling her hands into fists.

"Surrender first!" The leader yelled. He marched over to Matt and pulled the revolver out. The gun clicked close to Matt's head. "You might be strong, but you're not faster than a bullet."

Mira looked at Matt, panic spreading over her face. She swallowed and dropped to her knees. The man holding the gun to Matt's head didn't move the weapon as he turned to another man. "Collar her."

The man with broken glasses walked up to Mira with what looked like a choker made of metal blocks with runes etched into the surface. He wrapped the thick collar around Mira's neck, locking it in place with a loud click. Mira flinched as the blocks touched her skin. The man roughly pulled her to her feet by her shoulder and ripped her face mask off to reveal her tusks.

"Shame," the leader snarled, stowing his gun away. "I was hoping your tusks would make better trophies."

"Leave her alone, you asshole!" Matt lashed out, swinging his legs.

"This one's got some fire!" The leader chuckled, looking back at Matt. "Bring him along. He might be useful."

Matt fought against his captor as he was carried to the van and thrown in the back with Mira. They were pushed up against one side of the van as the other Oak Hand agents climbed in after them. Matt watched the agents angrily but knew he couldn't fight them off if they had guns. Mira was sitting next to him, pale and breathing heavily.

"Mira?" Matt asked. "Mira, what's wrong?"

"Fae iron," one of the agents grunted. "Makes the cockroaches weaker."

"She's in pain! We're cooperating, just take it off!"

"The minute we do? She'll kill us all. Trust me, this is for everyone's safety."

"She wasn't hurting anyone before you showed up!" Matt reeled.

"Keep it down back there!" The leader ordered from the front seat. "No more chatter."

The rest of the ride was silent. One of the Oak Hand agents was nursing a broken nose and had discarded the sunglasses that Mira had broken. Matt figured it was better not to antagonize the agents, since he was outnumbered and easily outmatched without Mira's help. Mira's focus was on the floor of the van, breathing through the pain around her neck.

Matt tried to track where they were moving through town, noting the turns and occasionally sneaking a glance out the window. If he could escape, he could run to the diner and get reinforcements. He knew the town well enough that he might be able to lose the van on foot, but he was reluctant to leave Mira alone. Matt guessed they were in the old shipping yard when the van came to a rough stop. They'd practically been right on top of the Oak Hand's hideout.

Mira was pulled out of the van first and Matt was clotheslined as he ran out after her. He felt less than heroic laying on the ground and looking up at the sky.

"Maybe we should have collared the runt, too?" An agent laughed as he pulled Matt to his feet by his shirt.

"Now, now," the leader smiled. "There's no need to be so rough with the boy. We're going to have a nice conversation with our new friend. And if he causes us any more trouble? We have plenty of ways to make him cooperate."

Chapter 11

LaBelle was walking to the troll stoneyard when his phone started ringing in his pocket. Any other phone wouldn't get a signal this far down, but LaBelle made the necessary enchantments to his phone for work purposes. He recognized the number, flipped the phone open, and answered. "Hello?"

"I can't find Mira," Dolly said, panicked. "She and Matt left for North Point earlier and I don't know where they are now."

"Try calling them," LaBelle said. "Did you give Mira a phone?"

"She's not answering. And I called Matt; he's not answering either. I sent Irene to check on them at the pier, but there's no sign of them there."

"They're teenagers, Dolly. I bet they're just messing around."

"No, I have a bad feeling, LaBelle. I can't see the future, but I have some sense of foresight. Something is very wrong."

"If anyone else told me this, I'd take it with a grain of salt. But you're sure they're in trouble?"

"I can feel it in my gut," Dolly urged. "I can't see specifics, but I'm worried."

"Alright," LaBelle groaned, running his hand down his face. "I'll go check out the pier. If that's where they said they were going, maybe I'll find a clue to where they went."

"Call me when you find them," Dolly urged.

"I'll bring them back to the diner as soon as I get them." LaBelle hung up the phone and slipped it back into his pocket. He let out a sharp exhale and grumbled. "Guess I'll take the express route."

Taking out his wand, LaBelle traced a leyline circle around himself and marked the floor with runes at the four points of the compass in a trail of glittering, blue light. LaBelle knelt on the cave floor and drew a smaller four-rune sigil ring, placing his wand at the center of his design. "Take me to the North Point Pier."

The circle glowed brighter and brighter until it flared like a flashbulb had gone off from the tip of LaBelle's wand. His vision shrank into a narrow passage that carried him through the leyline network that spiderwebbed throughout the city. Traveling this way was faster, but disorienting for most people. Even LaBelle didn't like using it because time, space, and the sense of his body were twisted and distorted in the magical pathways that tossed LaBelle's consciousness around between powerful landmarks in the area.

There was another flash of light and LaBelle's vision cleared up on the shores of the North Point Beach. Waves crashed against the sand and LaBelle was reminded of stepping off the ship for a few days on shore leave with crew mates. The smell of the sea spray reminded him of traveling the oceans, singing in over a dozen languages while he worked through the years.

As a giant Irish wolfhound lumbered up to him with a ball, LaBelle kicked some of the sand to hide the burn marks of his entrance. The dog came and sniffed his open hand, licking his fingers. LaBelle grinned and patted the dog's neck. "Hey, boy, any chance you've seen a misplaced troll and her stray human?"

The wolfhound looked towards the pier and rushed back toward his owners. LaBelle looked to the wooden dock and saw two sets of shoe prints, still clear in the moist sand by the water as the tide pulled out. LaBelle followed the trail until he was under the pier where the footprints blurred into the surf. He tried to make sense of the overlapping footsteps when he heard a splash and looked up in time to see a dark green form hide behind a beam.

"I know you're there," LaBelle announced, clearly. "Come out now. I swear by the Fae Queen, I offer you no harm."

The mermaid peered out from her hiding place, cautious. LaBelle smiled and bowed deeply before taking a few steps closer. "What's your name?"

"Tika," the mermaid replied quietly.

"Where are you from, Tika?"

"My father is of the Southern Gulf Pod," Tika slipped through the surf and crawled closer to the shoreline. "And my mother is from the Caribbean."

"Caribbean? Do you know anyone in the Cal Caribbean Pod by chance?"

"That's my mother's pod!" Tika perked up.

"I thought as much. That little splash of blue under your eyes gives it away. It sets your pod apart from most mid-Atlantic merfolk. I haven't seen any of the Cal-Caribbean pod since I was pirating in Tortuga."

"Tortuga? The Cal-Caribbean Pod hasn't been in the old pirating ports for ages."

"I have the privilege of living a longer and more diverse life than most in this world can claim," LaBelle said. "I don't suppose you've seen a half-troll girl recently?"

"With the human friend?"

"So they were here."

"They came asking for a prophecy, but I couldn't tell them anything," Tika rubbed her hands. "The troll got upset."

"I'm sorry it came to that," LaBelle frowned. "I'll have to have a word with her when I find them. Did you see where they went?"

"They were up there," Tika pointed to the boardwalk. "There was yelling and I heard a loud crash. I saw the human—Matt—try to fight them, but there were too many and they were kidnapped."

"The Oak Hand?"

"I assumed."

"Shit," LaBelle cursed. "Did you see where they went?"

"Last I saw them was over there," Tika said, pointing further down the shore. "When I heard the yelling, I watched from a distance. They took them to the forsaken place. My queen has me watch it, but I'm not supposed to get too close."

"Sounds like your queen has been watching the Oak Hand," LaBelle said. "Can you lead me there?"

"This way!" Tika splashed into the water and LaBelle could see the waves cut by her large dorsal fin. LaBelle drew two, quick sigil rings around the soles of his shoes and rushed after her without breaking the surface of the water. Tika would breach occasionally to ensure LaBelle was following her, but he was never more than a step or two behind. Tika turned sharply to the left and LaBelle followed her back to the shore, stepping onto the sand and kneeling by some boulders half-covered in seaweed. Tika climbed ashore, hiding behind the rocks next to LaBelle.

"There," Tika said. "They brought the van to that door, took Matt and Mira out, and then drove the van to the parking lot there."

"Has anyone come out? Other vans or boats?"

"Nothing I've seen," Tika shook her head. "For what it's worth? I hope they're OK."

"So do I," LaBelle frowned. "If they're not, I'm gonna have some very angry trolls after me. You should get somewhere safe. I'm sure a mermaid is high on the Oak Hand's trophy list."

"You don't have to tell me twice," Tika frowned. "Good luck." Pulling herself back into the water, Tika slid under the sea foam and let the tide carry her away.

LaBelle looked at the warehouse and rubbed his cheek. He'd known about an Oak Hand base by the pier but hoped it would be inactive. It wasn't a fortress by any stretch of the imagination, but one mistake could cost Mira or Matt their lives. Carefully, LaBelle started thinking of a plan.

The warehouse was a long building with steel beams and walls of aluminum-covered plywood to protect the crates inside from the elements. Towers of boxes filled the main warehouse, but Matt and Mira were carried across the big, concrete floor towards a series of administrative offices. Matt looked around and saw a target range set up with crude drawings of fairies, vampires, wizards, and trolls that had bullet holes or knives stuck in their foreheads.

The Oak Hand agent carried Matt into the warehouse and brought him and Mira into the third office down the hall. Mira fell on the floor when he dropped her, but Matt had to be taped into the office chair by one of the other agents. After he was securely restrained, the Oak Hand left them alone.

Across from Matt's involuntary seat, there was an aluminum desk and a map of Hedgefield with small, red dots all over it. Matt's stomach turned when he saw a jar on the desk containing a fairy suspended in alcohol that was caught in her last desperate moments of life. Mira was lying on the floor with her hands tied behind her, too weak from the Fae Iron collar to stand.

"Mira?" Matt whispered, trying to pull his legs and arms free. "Mira!"

The half-troll stirred on the ground, but couldn't do much more than look up at Matt sadly. "I'm sorry."

"You don't have to be sorry," Matt said. "We'll get our sorries out when we bust out of here."

"They're going to kill me."

"Don't talk like—"

"No, listen to me, Matt!" Mira urged, her voice hoarse. "Not many Underfolk escape the Oak Hand. And those that do, don't come back the same. I'm going to die. And they're going to give you a choice."

"What choice?"

"They'll want you to join them. Either you join the Oak Hand or they kill you. And I want you to take their offer."

"Mira, I'd never—"

"I'm already dead, Matt," Mira whimpered on the floor. "You might as well make it out of here alive."

"I'm not gonna leave you here to die. We get out together or not at all."

"Why? You barely know me."

"I know enough. You're a good person and these guys are just a bunch of bullies with guns! I may barely know you, but I know enough about them. You're my friend and I don't leave friends behind. So if they want to hurt you, they'll have to hurt me first."

"That's what I'm worried about," Mira said, her eyes welling up with tears. "If this is how it ends? I'm glad you're here with me. You're a good friend."

"I just wish I could have done more."

The door opened and the leader of the group marched in with another agent. He scowled at Matt and looked down at Mira on the floor. "Take her to the other room," the leader said. "We'll sort her out soon enough."

"No, no!" Mira cried as an agent grabbed her roughly by the ankle and dragged her out of the room. "Matt!"

"Mira! I'm gonna get you out of this!" Matt yelled, struggling against the bonds that held him in place. The heavy, iron door slammed and Matt watched hopelessly as he heard Mira being taken away down the hall. As the sounds faded, the Oak Hand commander walked over and set his gun on the aluminum table before sitting on the edge of the desk.

"Now then," the commander grinned, sitting across from Matt. "Let's figure out where you fit into all this. My name is Captain Marshall Lane. What's yours?"

"Let us go now!" Matt said, panic making the plea taste bitter. "We'll leave you alone, I swear! Just don't hurt her, she hasn't done anything!"

"You think that monster wasn't going to kill you the first chance it got?"

"Mira is my friend!"

"It's been using you," Captain Lane shook his head. "From day one. That thing tricked you into helping it. Three of our guys pursued that monster into the grocery store and we know it forced you to help. We know it made you lie to the police for it, drive it around, and God knows what else. If it's threatening you, we can protect you and your family."

"I chose to help Mira. And I'm glad I did!"

"How long have you known it? A day, day and a half? My men and I have been hunting these monsters for longer than you've been alive. The minute that thing loses its temper? It'll tear you in half."

"She'd never hurt me."

"I don't think you get it," Captain Lane scoffed. "We just saved your life! That thing would kill you if you blink at it wrong."

"Of the two of you? She hasn't held a gun to my head."

"Oh, did you really think I was gonna do anything?" Captain Lane asked. "Listen, uh…shit, I don't know your name."

"Matt."

"Matt," Captain Lane said, calmly. "Look, I just want to set the record straight: I love this world. I love humanity. And it's parasites like that thing—"

"Her name is Mira!" Matt snarled.

"That monster is just the beginning!" Captain Lane roared and pointed towards the door. "One or two and no one notices, but what happens when they come to take what they see as theirs? Some of us are privileged enough to know that once we were nothing but sport for those monsters. Ages ago, we made a deal with those things: we get the Above and they stay in the dirt where they belong. They break that deal every day. Someone has to show them what happens when they do."

Captain Lane shifted on the desk and picked up the jar with the fairy inside. He held it up, examining it in the light with a slight grin. "Take this little beastie here," Captain Lane said. "Alone? It isn't much more of a nuisance than a housefly, but you get enough of these together and they'll curse people just for walking by. There are tales of fairies making deals with humans only to take their deepest wish and twist it into torture. Now imagine a whole world of these things or worse! That's what I want to prevent. If it weren't for the Oak Hand, we'd be overrun in weeks. It's because of us that humanity is free. Wouldn't you say that killing this fairy was the right thing to do for humanity?"

"I suppose that depends on if you ask the fairy," Matt said, cold. "Mira asked for my help and I gave it to her. She's given me more chances to walk away than I can count, but I stayed because I wanted to. You were the ones who kidnapped us and you want me to believe your story? You can sit there all day and tell me that you're the good guys, but I don't buy it."

"Well, I'm sorry you feel that way," Captain Lane said, setting the jar back with a sigh. "Believe me or not, I'm on your side. I think you have potential, Matt! You could be a valuable agent of the Oak Hand! We do more than hunt. We can give you resources to succeed: go to college and get a position with real influence! Imagine a city councilman who knew about the threat of the Underfolk? Imagine if you were the first mayor to clean out the plague right beneath our feet. You would make a valuable asset, even if you don't want to fight. You can do something that would help humanity. It's a thankless job, but the effort is worth every minute of peace."

"And if I refuse?"

"Well, our organization depends on secrecy. And if there's one thing I can't stand more than a cockroach, it's a traitor. Would you rather be a hero or a villain? It's an easy choice for me."

"Great pitch," Matt sneered. "Agree with me or die? And how do you know that I won't expose you? I might not be able to save Mira today, but I can still stop you."

"You're welcome to try, but do you think we'd let you walk away without keeping an eye on you? Besides, who would believe you?"

"You're wrong about Mira, about the Underfolk, and you're wrong about me."

"If that's too hard a decision for you to make, let me rephrase it: either you shoot that abomination or the last thing it'll see is us killing you. What's your preference, Matt?"

Matt's heart pounded in his chest and he felt like he was going to throw up. Captain Lane was tactical, strategic, and careful. While he had a passionate exterior, Matt was sure everything Lane did had a reason and this was why he had taken Matt. Even if LaBelle was going to wipe Matt's memory, he had valuable information to the Oak Hand now and Lane knew it. The knowledge in Matt's head made him a liability until it was taken out of the equation. The Council or even LaBelle might decide Matt had seen too much and just remove the problem entirely. He was a threat to the Under as long as he was alive and that meant Matt was in danger with what he knew. The Oak Hand's offer to protect him extended beyond just the Underfolk he knew about. But there were good people like Mira and Dolly. Matt knew there were good and bad people on both sides of the Oak Hand's self-righteous war, but he refused to be the judge. Anyone could be good or bad, but the Oak Hand chose to hurt. That wasn't who Matt wanted to be.

He took a final deep breath and looked up at Captain Lane, sternly. "Go to hell."

Captain Lane stood from the desk and brushed his hands on his pants. "I'll give you some time to think on it. She dies in ten minutes. Either you pull the trigger or you die in nine."

Chapter 12

Slipping through the open skylight, LaBelle stepped onto one of the high stacks of boxes. He had his wand drawn and ready, casting a quick spell to muffle the sounds of his footsteps on the wooden crates. Casting an invisibility spell would take all his concentration and LaBelle knew that hiding his body without magic was easier than controlling all the sounds he made in the environment. He was examining the layout of the room when he saw a man dragging Mira's limp body out of an office. The Oak Hand agent pushed her into an office and slammed the door behind her. LaBelle tried to judge the distance to the ground and decided it would be easier to sneak through the rafters.

"Hey!" An agent with a gun shouted, pointing at him. "Stop right —!"

The vision froze once he'd been caught and slowly disappeared until LaBelle was back on the beach, hiding behind the rock.

"Damn," LaBelle blinked, slipping out of the future trance. Looking down, LaBelle consulted the map he'd drawn in the sand. He ran an 'X' through the skylight and scratched it off his mental list of possibilities. That was all eight windows, both doors, the loading bay, and the rooftop window he'd found in his exploratory missions through the Veil. Each time he tried to plan his infiltration, he'd learned a little more, but it still wasn't enough to get in, grab the kids, and disappear without all five of the Oak Hand agents coming down on the three of them.

LaBelle had used every spell he could think of to find a way in. It was hardly a fortress, but the Oak Hand was vigilant and the confrontation was impossible to avoid so far. The visions of potential rescues were more useful for reconnaissance since he kept finding ways to get caught. He'd hoped that one would be successful, but nothing he'd thought of so far got him in and out without the entire warehouse attacking him or hurting one of the kids.

"Well," LaBelle sighed, kicking the sand and clearing his map. "I guess there's only one option."

LaBelle walked up from the beach, striding along the concrete sidewalk over to the warehouse. Putting his hands in his pockets, LaBelle casually strolled down the waterfront and up to the door under a lone, yellow lamp that flickered a little. He took one hand out of his pocket and knocked on the door.

A small slit in the door opened and a pair of angry eyes glared at him. "What do you want?"

"Good afternoon," LaBelle grinned. "I've spent a good deal of time over on that beach trying to figure out a way to sneak in without leading to violence. I gotta admit, you have me stumped! So, I figured —since you were going to notice me no matter what—I should just come and ask politely."

"Why should I care?"

"Listen, there's a couple of teenagers inside and I need to get them home unharmed. The best solution is you just hand them over and we all go our separate ways. I'm even willing to give you a two-day head start to clear out of the building before I come back. Fair?"

"Piss off."

"Tell your boss that Blanc LaBelle is here."

"He'd say piss off, too."

The eye slot in the door slammed shut and LaBelle sighed. He took another look at the door and frowned before getting the book from the holster at his ribs. Flipping through the pages, LaBelle found the runes he was looking for and checked the door again, assuring himself it would work. After he stashed the book back, he pulled out his wand and checked his watch. "Well, at least I asked nicely first," LaBelle said and pointed his wand at the door. "Time's up, boys."

LaBelle rotated his wrist, drawing a circle of light on the door with the tip of his wand and then drawing the four runes along the edge of the sigil ring. He released the spell and the metal door crashed into the warehouse, ripping out part of the frame with it. Adjusting his suit coat, LaBelle strode through the opening and fired a quick bolt of energy at the doorman. The Oak Hand agent was thrown from his feet and crashed through the wood of a large crate full of straw. LaBelle could hear a commotion inside and moved into the open warehouse.

"Knock knock! LaBelle's delivery service!"

Four men rushed into the room, confirming the count he'd made from his earlier visions. That meant he'd made enough of an entrance to attract everyone but one of the Oak Hand agents. If they were all coming for him, it meant the kids were safe so far. Matt and Mira were only sixteen, but LaBelle was a more than competent opponent for these crusaders.

With a two-rune sigil, LaBelle filled the room with a thick, gray fog and then cast a spell on his feet to silence his footsteps. He smiled, thinking of when had used this technique with a vampire while hunting Nazi magi in World War II. When he moved through the mist, LaBelle barely disturbed the air around him and he passed by the men swinging their guns around to any sound they heard. Other wizards would be familiar with the spell, but LaBelle had the advantage in this room of panicked humans. Sneaking up on one man from behind, he quickly cast a one-rune spell and slashed his wand across the agent's throat, splattering blood on the floor.

"He's over here!" A man yelled and started shooting. LaBelle ran for the cover of the stacked crates and dissipated the mist around him. He drew a three-rune sigil in the air and the bullets congregated at the tip of his wand like a ball of angry, metal bees. While he was fighting in the American Revolution, he'd learned this trick from a sorcerer when they were under heavy fire. The more bullets that were shot at LaBelle, the more mass for the cannonball LaBelle intended to fire back. Footsteps tipped LaBelle off to the agent trying to surprise him from behind. With a quick flick of his wand, LaBelle's bullet ball went through the chest of the would-be attacker, leaving him as a crumpled heap against one of the warehouse walls.

"Go! Get Lane!" One of the two remaining agents yelled. The younger man ran off down the hallway, leaving LaBelle with the last fighter willing to face him. The Oak Hand agent dropped his empty pistol and drew a long, iron knife from the sheath on his ankle. LaBelle wrapped his hand around the end of his wand and pulled, drawing his wand out into the shape of a long, falchion.

"Fourteen years on a pirate ship," LaBelle said, waving the point menacingly, "another twenty in the Roman Army, and add fifteen years invading Britain with the Vikings. Let's see if my experience is still a match for your eagerness."

LaBelle attacked quickly, using the width and length of his sword to his advantage. His most recent training with a blade was geared toward French fencing and so he kept correcting his form for the agent's undisciplined violence. LaBelle enjoyed the challenges that came with each unique opponent and drew out the fight to better understand exactly what the Oak Hand was teaching their recruits. "Come on," LaBelle said, grinning as the blades clashed. "That's it, mind your stance! Don't lose your footing for the sake of a powerful swing!"

The Oak Hand agent swung his knife at LaBelle's stomach, but the detective blocked the attack and slashed upward, cutting the man's stomach with a flourish. The falchion faded away, leaving LaBelle with just his wand. The Oak Hand agent collapsed behind him, leaving a red stain on the floor. LaBelle walked slowly down the hall where he'd seen the last agent run earlier. The lights were off and the corridor was pitch black.

LaBelle had spent time with werewolves. He'd hunted monsters that could see when he couldn't, so the werewolves taught him how to use his other senses. When sight and hearing failed him, LaBelle felt he could always count on his sense of smell. He wasn't as accurate at tracking as those who had taught him, but he was skilled enough to smell the sweat on the agent's brow as he approached. LaBelle reached out with his left hand and grabbed the hiding man by the soft flesh of his neck. A quick twist and the man dropped to the floor with a chunk of his throat missing. He choked and gurgled as blood filled his mouth. The agent couldn't scream, so he wheezed on the floor clutching at his neck until he was out of breath.

Turning to the closest door, LaBelle struggled with the handle. He took out his wand, drew a one-rune sigil, and tapped the lock with his spell. The door clicked and LaBelle kicked it open with his wand drawn.

"Mira!" LaBelle rushed over to her on the floor of the storeroom with a Fae Iron collar choking her. LaBelle touched the tip of his wand to the iron band and the metal melted away as sand. Mira coughed and gasped for air as if her lungs had just started working again. "Breathe, just breathe," LaBelle rubbed her back and watched the door. "Where's Matt?"

"He's down the hall," Mira rasped.

"Can you walk?"

Mira nodded and stood. She took the lead and LaBelle followed, stopping her as they approached the door and pushing her out of the way. He cast another two-rune sigil and the door unlocked. LaBelle forced his way through, but put a hand out to stop Mira from rushing in.

"Drop your wand!" An older Oak Hand agent yelled, hiding behind Matt with a gun on his neck. "Drop it or he dies!"

LaBelle held up his wand and set it on the floor. He felt Mira take a step and stopped her from charging into the room. "It doesn't have to end like this," LaBelle pleaded with the commander. "You can walk away from this and no one else has to get hurt."

"I have an alternative!" The commander yelled, pressing the gun closer to Matt's head. "First, I kill him! Then I kill you and I end things by killing that filthy monster!"

LaBelle let out a breath and flexed his empty hands. He could feel the energy building, filling the space between his fingers. All he had to do was find the right thread of magic. "Please," LaBelle said, calmly, "don't do this."

"You killed my men!"

"And they killed Underfolk." Thunder rumbled overhead as LaBelle found the thread he was looking for and hooked it around his finger. "They wore murder on their hearts like a badge of honor."

"They defended their rights! They died to defend humanity from you monsters! And I swear, I won't stop until every last one of you is —"

The room exploded with sound and light as LaBelle tugged on the magical thread he'd grabbed like it was the trigger on a gun. He winced and turned from the flash and instantly smelled burning hair and flesh. The lightning faded and LaBelle blinked a little to refocus. When the spots faded from his vision, LaBelle saw the commander's body splayed out on the floor with his back split open and smoldering. Matt was still standing but trembled as the ringing in everyone's ears died down.

"Matt!" Mira rushed over and hugged him. "Are you okay?"

"Yeah, I think so," Matt stammered out, looking at his hands to ensure everything was still attached.

"We need to get out of here, now!" LaBelle ordered, picking up his wand. "The longer we're here, the more likely the Oak Hand will send their people to investigate when these guys don't check-in."

"What about him?" Matt asked, pointing to the commander. "Is he dead?"

"As dead as the rest of them in the main warehouse," LaBelle said, drawing a leyline circle on the floor. "Let's go!"

"What about the bodies?" Matt asked.

"What about them?" LaBelle asked.

"We can't just leave a warehouse full of dead bodies!" Matt snapped.

LaBelle frowned, grabbed another thread of magic, and shot a fireball at the fairy in the jar on the desk. The glass shattered and alcohol caught fire quickly, spreading up the map on the wall and lighting insulation on fire. "There," LaBelle said, finishing the leyline circle. "Tragic scenario: freak lightning struck the building, rags caught on fire, and these poor souls were trapped in the blaze. What a shame. Now, let's go!"

"Wait, we can't—"

"You are in no position to argue with me now," LaBelle snarled. "I'm saving the height of my anger for when you're both safely at Dolly's again. Move it!"

"We can't pretend this didn't happen! What about the police?"

"We'll arrange a cover-up," LaBelle growled. "I'm more worried about you two. Now, get in the circle!"

Matt looked between LaBelle and the carnage on the floor around him. The building was already starting to burn and the detective eyed him carefully, already preparing for the next argument. Mira took Matt's hand and looked at him. "Matt, please, I don't want to be here anymore."

"Okay," Matt said, looking at LaBelle again, "but I don't like this."

"You'd like the alternative worse," LaBelle said, motioning Mira and Matt into the circle with him. He drew the center sigil rune and faced it west. "Take us to Dolly's."

The circle glowed for a moment and the trio was pulled through the leylines that were laced over the city. The world narrowed for a minute and LaBelle's circle carried them to an alley behind Dolly's diner. LaBelle straightened out his jacket but paused when he heard vomiting behind him.

"Deep breaths, Mira," LaBelle suggested, sliding his wand back into his holster. "First time using a leyline circle can be rough."

"That was Matt," Mira said.

LaBelle turned and saw Mira rubbing Matt's back as he wiped his mouth. The detective rolled his eyes and let out a long breath. "Both of you get in the diner."

"LaBelle—"

"Mira! You'll have a chance to apologize after we've discussed this, but I'd rather do that once you're safely inside. Now!"

Mira nodded and quickly walked ahead of LaBelle with Matt following close behind her. Dolly perked up when everyone came in, but LaBelle shook his head and the centaur settled. He ushered Mira and Matt upstairs and into the half-troll's room. Closing the door behind him and folding his arms, LaBelle's next question was a roll of thunder that preceded a storm. "Alright, what happened?"

Chapter 13

"—and then Matt and I got separated," Mira said. LaBelle had listened to her story, occasionally interrupting for details but mostly letting his disapproval simmer. "They just left me in that room and I thought I was about to die when you came in."

"And you?" LaBelle asked, looking at Matt.

"Captain Lane was giving me this whole speech about the Oak Hand," Matt said. "He wanted me to join them and said he'd kill me if I didn't."

"Did you?"

"Why would I—?"

"Did you?" LaBelle repeated, firmer.

Matt shook his head and dropped his shoulders a bit. "I told him to go to hell. He said he was gonna kill me and then kill Mira. Then you came in after a bunch of fighting."

"Good," LaBelle said. "Now that I've heard your side of the story, I have a question to start: what were you thinking, Mira?"

"I didn't—"

"You told me to stay with Mira," Matt said, jumping to her defense. "We were safe—"

"Clearly, she wasn't safe!" LaBelle yelled. He pinched the bridge of his nose and sighed. "I told you to stay with her, not to be her valet into Oak Hand-infested docks!"

"Matt and I didn't know about—"

"You both should have assumed!" LaBelle dragged his hand down his face. "Mira, you could have been killed! And for a mermaid's prophecy?"

"I didn't—" Mira sniffled. "I didn't think it would be bad. I thought it would help."

"Mira, if I thought that, I would have gone myself!" LaBelle said. "Prophecies are unreliable and I have ways of getting more accurate ones. You asked me to find your father and I'm working on it, but you have to trust that I know what I'm doing!"

"I was just trying to help," Mira wiped her eyes with the back of her hand. "I'm sorry."

"Dural is already demanding you be returned to your clan. If he finds out you were taken by the Oak Hand, he'd want you back tonight."

"So, you're not gonna tell him?" Mira asked.

"Not yet," LaBelle sighed. "I did say I would find your father and I mean to keep that promise. But no more leeway, understood? Another step out of line and I'll carry you back to the troll caves over my shoulder, if I have to. You're going to stay in this room or work in the diner with Dolly unless I say otherwise. Am I clear?"

"Yes sir," Mira nodded, looking at her hands in her lap.

"And you!" LaBelle snapped, pointing at Matt. "You're too much of a liability to be out and about. You come here in the morning, then go straight home where your parents can keep an eye on you. I'd rather have you sleep here, but deviating too far from appearances would raise more suspicions than I want."

"I can stay?" Matt asked.

"You made an impossible choice," LaBelle affirmed, calmer. "I wouldn't wish that kind of decision on anyone. You held strong when you were in danger and you were loyal. A lot of people would say anything to survive."

"I don't like to lie."

"Lying comes easily to humans," LaBelle said, "but you weren't lying about what you said. You were willing to die rather than join the Oak Hand. I'm not saying you deserve to be a saint yet, but I trust you enough to stay with Mira. I'd rather she not be alone. If the Oak Hand found her twice by luck, that's too many coincidences for comfort. I'm going to talk with Dolly."

"LaBelle?" Mira started. She waited for him to nod with the hope of not making the situation worse. "When we talked to the mermaid she said that my father's face was obscured in her vision. Does that mean anything?"

"It could," LaBelle thought, shifting into the investigator part of his mind. "The number of Underfolk who could block out their identity from a vision is limited and if a human had their face hidden? I'd bet that's a very short list. I can consult with another source that might be able to give me that information. I wish you'd asked permission first, but I can appreciate what you learned. I'll find out more tomorrow."

"What about my car?" Matt piped in.

LaBelle took a deep breath and scowled at Matt. "I'll get your car back before you need to leave tonight. Any other stupid questions?"

Matt didn't say anything and Mira shook her head, staring down at her feet. "Good," LaBelle said. "I'm going to talk to Dolly downstairs. I'm guessing I don't have to stress this, but don't do anything else that might get one of you killed!"

LaBelle left the room and slammed the door behind him. There was a moment of stillness and Matt looked at Mira with a smile. "I thought he'd be angrier."

"Matt, were you really willing to let them hurt you?"

"I don't like bullies. Those guys are pointlessly cruel."

"I was so scared," Mira's voice shook. Thinking about being powerless on the floor of the warehouse made her whole body tense and her heart pounded in her chest. "The only thing I could think was that you were going to get hurt because of something I did and I was —"

"Mira, if anyone got me hurt, it wouldn't have been your fault. If someone threatens me because of who you are, they're the ones who make that choice. They held a gun to my head, but I know you'd never hurt me."

Mira wiped her eyes and blinked out a few tears. "Thanks for being a good friend."

"Are you okay?" Matt asked. "When they took you—"

"I don't want to talk about it."

"Mira…"

"Just hold me?"

Matt put an arm around Mira's shoulder and held her close to him. She pushed her face into Matt's chest and shuddered a little. Matt moved back on the bed so their backs were resting against the window and he ran his fingertips along her upper arm. Mira pressed her face further into Matt's chest and inhaled. He smelled like the sea.

"They're not going to hurt you, Mira," Matt said. "I promise."

Mira's body shook with big sobs as the stress of the ordeal finally broke her. She felt safe in Matt's arms, but the thought of someone hating her so much baffled her and made her more upset. Mira sniffled and burrowed deeper into Matt's shoulder, wrapping her arms around his neck. She tucked her knees close to her chest and scooted closer. "Tell me a story," Mira said. "Anything to get me out of that room with the collar around my neck."

Matt held Mira close to his body. For a minute, Mira worried he didn't want to say anything, but he started talking quietly. "A few years ago," Matt said, "my friends—Drew, Whitney, and Nico—and I all went out to Rein Island together. We rented kayaks, paddled out, and beached the boats on the island. It was the peak of summer and the tourists wanted to avoid the creepy hotel so we had the whole beach to ourselves. We swam in the ocean and lounged by the water all day. Drew and I even went into the abandoned hotel. It's supposed to be haunted, but he dared me to go in with him. We walked together and started looking in every room. Drew was looking for something to give to Whitney to prove he wasn't a coward, but I kept expecting ghosts to jump out of the closets. I nearly jumped out of my skin when a rat rushed by our feet, but I wasn't gonna go running out before Drew."

"I don't want Mira leaving the diner without me again." LaBelle sat at the counter with a huff. "She's had a rough day, but she'll live."

"What happened?" Dolly asked.

"Oak Hand," LaBelle grumbled. "There were five of them. Let's just say that the issue has been resolved."

"By the River," Dolly gasped and put a hand on her chest. "And the kids are safe?"

"I got there fast enough," LaBelle said. "If it hadn't been for you, I don't know if we would have been as lucky."

"That poor girl," Dolly said, looking towards the rooms. "I'm giving her the night off, she needs it."

"How could they have been so stupid?" LaBelle cursed, nearly knocking over a coffee cup with a swing of his arm. Dolly caught the mug and started filling it. "Of all the irresponsible things! What was she expecting? How could Mira be so naive about the Above? If I hadn't shown up, she might not have survived. "

"It takes time to learn these things. She's been in the Above two, maybe three days?"

"She should have known better!"

"And you should direct some of that anger at the Oak Hand!" Dolly snapped, turning and walking over to the small window that separated the kitchen from the rest of the restaurant. "Or maybe the Council! What have they ever done about the Oak Hand? The Magi Prima could wipe them out with a wave of their wands. Hell, you could do it with less effort!"

"And then what? I've fought and wiped out organizations like that before, but ideologies are harder to kill. I mean, she came to me running from the Oak Hand. Just because she got bored of waiting doesn't mean that there isn't still a threat!"

"I didn't even know about the North Pier hideout. Did you tell her?"

"What does that matter?"

"You can't keep expecting her to know all the rules of the Above," Dolly insisted, coming back with a plate of steak and eggs. "She's sixteen and hasn't been up in the Above before. Is it her fault that she wants to feel safe going outside and exploring a little?"

"I'm not saying it's her fault, but—" LaBelle struggled. "I can't help her if I'm babysitting. I didn't think I'd have to explain that she'd have to be so careful in the human world."

"It's a lesson she had to learn the hard way," Dolly said. "And hopefully once. She's back now. Let's be glad of that and get her somewhere to call home."

"The sooner, the better."

LaBelle ate his dinner in silence, taking out a notebook and writing down what he knew so far. Dolly kept the coffee warm but didn't bother him any further. LaBelle made a few notes from his visit down to the troll caves and jotted down the results of the attack at the Oak Hand base. After he finished, LaBelle stood and tipped back his coffee with a final swig.

"Do me a favor," LaBelle said, putting his hat back on. "Don't let her leave the diner."

"She's not a prisoner," Dolly said, "but I'll discourage her from further adventures when I bring her up some food in a bit."

"Mmm," LaBelle nodded. "Put it on my tab."

LaBelle left the diner and went back to his office. On the walk back, he could only mull over the number of people he knew who would be hidden from a fae's vision. He'd done it himself for friends before, but only in very serious situations. LaBelle had rarely heard of a human hidden from the fae's sight, but the Fae Queen rarely liked when secrets were kept from her. He figured that she would have a list of names he could look at, but she would be too covetous of such things that he would be better off asking elsewhere.

Entering his office, LaBelle was surprised by a small, green humanoid with big ears standing by his desk. The goblin only came up to LaBelle's knee and grinned with a mouthful of fangs that put LaBelle on edge. The big, yellow eyes looked up at him, in fear or adoration, LaBelle didn't know.

"I'm not taking new cases at the moment," LaBelle grumbled. "If you'd like, I know some Underfolk who—"

"Not looking for help," the goblin said in a gravelly voice, "Goblin Falee looking to help you, the LaBelle."

"I don't do consultants," LaBelle said, annoyed. "I have more than enough contacts to—"

"A gift from Troll Mayza," Falee said, reaching into their pocket. "A gift for the LaBelle."

Falee extended their hand, holding out a folded bundle of cloth. LaBelle bent over, took the parcel from the goblin, and unfolded it in his hand. The necklace was a gold chain that had a round pendant marked with runes and dotted with green gemstones. With a blur, LaBelle grabbed the goblin's ratty vest and lifted them against the wall. "Where did you get this?" LaBelle yelled. "How did you—?"

"Troll Mayza!" Falee pleaded, cowering. "Goblin Falee did not steal! No harm, no harm!"

LaBelle glowered and looked down at the necklace in his grip. He dropped the goblin and glared. "Get out."

Falee rushed off and scrambled out through the office window, scampering down the fire escape. Once he was alone, LaBelle recovered from the shock and turned the necklace over in his hands. The pattern of the sigil and the spacing of the gems were too specific. He could feel the magic radiating: illusion and disguise.

"Snap out of it, LaBelle!" He sat at his desk and rubbed his face. "It's just a glamour token! They're a dime a dozen in the Under. Hell, you've made them before."

The feeling still bothered him, like an insect bite in the back of his mind. LaBelle ran his thumb along the edge of the pendant and frowned. He put the jewelry in a drawer and brought his focus back to the case, looking up and turning his back to the desk.

"Alright," LaBelle thought to himself aloud and physically shaking off the distraction. "Mira's father is someone important to the Underfolk, not just a random Joe on the street. And he's a, uh…not someone that Kaysar talked about a lot, but someone who…"

The thoughts all drifted back to the same conclusion. It felt wrong to say it and LaBelle leaned back in his chair. "Damn it, Kate," LaBelle shook his head. "What'd you get yourself into?"

<u>Chapter 14</u>

"Thought you two might be hungry," Dolly said, opening the door and picking up the tray behind her.

Mira looked up from Matt's shoulder and smiled. Dolly had come up with a tray carrying two glasses of milk, a plate with a cheeseburger and fries, and another plate with a full fried chicken on it. Dolly set the plates on top of the bureau by the door. "LaBelle may have you on lockdown, but I'm not going to feed you like prisoners."

"Thanks," Mira said. "I'll be down after—"

"Don't be silly," Dolly said, giving Matt the cheeseburger plate. "You had a traumatic experience and you deserve a rest. Are you okay?"

"For now," Mira said. "I just need time to recover."

"I'm just glad you're both home," Dolly handed Mira the chicken and rested a hand on her shoulder. "Now, LaBelle said you're not supposed to leave, but I don't want you to feel trapped. If you want to go outside again, I know some spots in the city that are safe and—"

"I honestly don't think I'm ready for another adventure right away. Besides, Matt's keeping me company."

"The world isn't all bad," Dolly said. "Maybe, now that LaBelle has cleared out that batch of bad apples, the pier will be a safe place for us."

"Hey, Dolly," Matt said, picking at some fries, "something has been bothering me. I know you're a centaur and Mira's a half-troll, but what is LaBelle?"

"You've never heard the stories of Blanc LaBelle?"

"Not until recently."

"I thought your grandma was a witch? I can't think of a single Underfolk who hasn't heard about LaBelle."

"I only heard of him in passing," Mira said, jumping to Matt's defense. "Even in the Under, we don't talk about him much. All I know is that most of the beasts aren't fond of him."

Dolly scrunched her face and folded her arms. "LaBelle is a question that no one wants to answer. He's older than most Underfolk. No one really knows how old, except for a select few."

"But is he a magi?" Mira asked. "He called lightning from the sky without a wand, but he seems to prefer using one."

"That's part of why LaBelle is hard to classify," Dolly said. "Matt, I assume your grandmother uses a wand or something else for casting spells?"

"Of course," Matt said, after an urgent look from Mira.

"And the Fae can pull magic from the energy around us," Dolly said, reaching out and pinching her fingers around something Matt couldn't see. She turned her wrist and a flame sparked at her fingertips. Matt tried to contain his reaction, but it was difficult not to show his amazement.

"But LaBelle?" Dolly said, extinguishing the flame. "He's something else entirely. If some of the older fae are to be believed, LaBelle has traveled all over the world and learned from every great magic wielder who has ever lived. But no one will say where LaBelle came from. If he's a magi, he's powerful beyond the scope of the Magi Prima. If he's fae, he's honed his power beyond even the Fae Queen."

"But you can do magic," Matt said.

"I can pull on threads of magic," Dolly corrected. "Even the most powerful fae can only draw on magic that already exists: elemental magic and magic related to the natural world. I can't conjure things like a magi or cast a spell to turn lead into gold. Some fae will make deals and use the desire of humans to get more power. I don't like fae deals, personally. They never work out for the humans and it's a painful compulsion for the fae involved. Our magic is limited by type and magi are limited by the rune sigils they know. LaBelle? He's something else entirely."

"I don't see how that earned him so much esteem among the beasts," Mira said.

"Esteem is a stretch," Dolly smiled. "Maybe understanding or perhaps even fear. He's earned the respect of a few, but only through painful trials. The Great Dragons distrust him since LaBelle is prophesied to kill Extoran, the Great Blue Dragon, and the last of dragon royalty. There are benefits to working together if only so we don't wipe each other out. LaBelle, in my opinion, is the one force that can maintain the peace between factions."

"The Council can't keep the peace?" Matt asked.

"They do," Dolly said, "but LaBelle is a source of justice. Since he doesn't fall cleanly into one category, he's an intermediary between factions. Or a spy, depending on who you ask."

"That's why he lives with the Fold," Mira said. "So, he doesn't have to choose one faction in the Under?"

"Those who live in the Above know we're few and far between. The Fold tends to stick together, but LaBelle is as close as we have to a leader. He feels more at home with those on the surface than any faction in the Under. He doesn't enforce any of the ancient laws, but he maintains order for those of us living here and makes sure humans don't fall into the Under. We can't go to the human police or the Council. Rather than leaving us to fend for ourselves, he protects us at an arm's length. That's why the Fold is strongest here in Hedgefield."

"So," Matt said, "he's not fae, he's not magi, and he's not a beast. What's left?"

"If you can answer that," Dolly smiled, "there are a lot of Underfolk who would love to know."

Dolly pulled Mira close and gave her a reassuring squeeze. "Wherever LaBelle is from? He's the best to solve your case. He'll find your dad and get you home safe."

"You think so?"

"I know so," Dolly grinned. "And next time you want a prophecy? Ask me first."

"I don't think I'll go looking for fae folk visions anytime soon," Mira said, "but I'll be down for the breakfast rush, I promise."

"Whenever you're ready, sweetie," Dolly said, kissing the top of Mira's head affectionately. "Take all the time you need."

Dolly left and closed the door behind her. Mira took her plate and sat across from Matt, cross-legged and crunching into a chicken wing. Matt picked at his fries but didn't eat any for a minute.

"It's not that I don't trust him," Matt said, "but can we guarantee that LaBelle has your best interests at heart?"

"I don't have a choice," Mira said, taking a drumstick off her plate. She crunched down, taking skin, flesh, and bone with a loud snap. Mira swallowed her bite and shrugged. "He's my best chance to find my father. I can trust him until I can think more than five minutes ahead."

Matt nodded and took a fry from his plate. "It's your turn to tell me a story," Matt said. "Something that you liked about living in the Under?"

Mira chewed for a minute and Matt thought she wasn't going to answer. He turned back to his plate in silence. He decided not to push for an answer but wanted to know all of Mira: the sorrows and joys that drove her.

"When I was young," Mira said. "My mother took me to see Fae Town. I hadn't seen magic before then, so walking into that part of the Under where it was so rampant was incredible. I spent time playing ball with the fae children and, for a little while, it felt like I was an actual kid for once. In the caves, it was all work and survival with little play for a lonely, half-troll child. I tried to hide from my mother when it was time to leave, but she started singing and I came out to find her."

"She sang?"

"Well, not what you'd consider singing. It's lower grumbles, I guess? Traditional troll lullabies are deeper than humans can hear. You feel it in the chest. It's less about the words than the feeling it evokes."

"That sounds like a lullaby to me," Matt said.

###

An hour later, LaBelle trudged back towards the diner. He had no further breakthroughs and he'd hit a final wall at the end of the day. He entered the diner using a key coin and gave Dolly a polite wave before heading up to the rooms. LaBelle walked to Mira's room and knocked on the door before coming in. Matt jumped off the bed and LaBelle had to hide a smile at Matt's reaction to being caught.

"Your car's out front."

"How did you get it here without the keys?" Matt asked, feeling the keys in his pockets.

"I can summon lightning, Matt. Hot-wiring a car isn't that difficult."

"I should probably get home," Matt said. "I told my mom I was working overtime, but that excuse will only last for so long."

"I'll wait for you to get here tomorrow before making my next move," LaBelle told him.

"What's the next move?" Mira asked.

"Figured I'd go straight to the source for a list of humans blocked from the fae's vision, but I doubt the Fae Queen will hand it over so easily. However, the sphinxes are obsessed with information—especially private information."

"The sphinxes?" Mira asked, standing eagerly. "Have you spoken to them before? What was the riddle they asked you?"

"If you want to know that," LaBelle smirked, "you'll have to ask them yourself sometime. Matt, I'll see you tomorrow."

Matt nodded, looked back to Mira, and hugged her. "I'll see you tomorrow."

"Thanks for keeping me company. Goodnight."

Matt walked over to the door and carefully squeezed passed LaBelle to go downstairs. LaBelle watched him go down the steps from the open door frame and frowned. "You should be careful. Don't let him get too close."

"He could have turned on me today," Mira said. "He didn't."

"The Oak Hand would have killed him for that."

"That's a reflection on them, not Matt. I take Matt at his word."

"You trust him, then?"

"So do you. You invited him to come back."

LaBelle turned back to Mira. "I have a question," LaBelle took the necklace out of his pocket. "Have you seen this before?"

"It was my mom's!" Mira said, reaching out and taking it. She smiled and ran her fingers along the edge of the medallion. "I thought it was gone forever when I left it behind. It was her glamour."

"You're sure she didn't get it from anyone else?"

"It wouldn't work for anyone else." Mira slipped the necklace around her neck and looked up at LaBelle unchanged, her troll features still prominent. "I've seen her use it once or twice, so it was designed for my mom. If I thought it would work for me, I'd have worn it to the Above."

LaBelle smiled, impressed. "You know about magic?"

"I'd peek in on magic classes on my way to and from my lessons growing up," Mira explained. "One of my tutors was an elf and they would let me read magic textbooks sometimes."

"Really?" LaBelle asked. "You had a tutor? Trolls aren't known for intellectual pursuits."

"Mom wanted me to learn more than the trolls could teach me," Mira said. "I can't cast any spells, but the books made good reading practice. My teachers taught me how to speak, read and write in

English. I also know a little French, but I don't speak it enough to call myself fluent."

"Your mom was thinking ahead."

"She knew I'd never be happy with the trolls," Mira said, looking down and running her fingers along the edge of the medallion. "I just wish that she was around long enough to tell me the rest of her plan."

"That makes two of us," LaBelle nodded. "I hope you're feeling better after today."

"I'll feel better when I find my dad."

"Then I'd better go to work," LaBelle nodded. "And if you want to keep working for Dolly tomorrow, you'd better get some rest."

Mira nodded and looked down at the pendant again. She took the necklace off and held it out to LaBelle. He shook his head and pushed it back to her. "You should keep it."

"Really?" Mira asked. "It won't work for me."

"It's important to you," LaBelle noted. "You should hold onto it for sentimental reasons."

"Trolls don't really believe in sentimentality."

"But you're only half-troll," LaBelle said.

Mira grinned a little and looked down at the pendant, a bit sad. She slipped the necklace around her neck and tucked the medallion into her shirt. "Thank you."

"You miss her, don't you?"

"I keep telling myself I got lucky," Mira swallowed. "That I got to be with her until the end and that she got to die in her home rather than in some skirmish with another troll. She was strong enough to die standing, even if she could barely breathe. I did all the grieving I thought I needed: I carried her to the stoneyard, I made her funeral rites with Mayza, and I wished her well on her journey to the Halls of her Forbearers. Still, there are some days I wish everything was a bad dream. I keep hoping that she's gonna come and wake me from a deep sleep to tell me that we need to go start with Mayza's morning chores. It feels like she's gone, but I keep waiting for her to come back to me."

"Speaking as something of a professional in watching people we love die?" LaBelle said. "It's never a simple checklist. Sometimes, the grief goes away long enough for you to keep moving on with your life. Other days, you want to harden your heart to the world so you don't have to feel anymore."

"How do you cope with it?" Mira asked.

"You let yourself feel it," LaBelle suggested. "It's never bad to miss someone. When you miss a person, a little bit of them lives on in you. When I was living with Vikings, we grieved and celebrated in the same breath. And, as long as we remembered and fought for the memory of those we lost? They never truly died. I still raise a glass to my fallen brothers in arms and they live on through me."

"Thanks, LaBelle," Mira said, collecting the plates. "That actually helps a little."

"Here," LaBelle took the plates from Mira, "let me get that."

"Are you sure?"

"I'm heading down through the diner already. Besides, Dolly will harass me if I don't start being nicer to you. I'll come back tomorrow before I leave."

"I'll try not to wander off." Mira smiled but turned serious after LaBelle looked at her sternly. "I was kidding."

"I'm sure you were," LaBelle shook his head with a grin. "Sleep well, Mira."

Chapter 15

Matt parked his car outside the apartment complex and blinked a few times. He'd been so wired between getting kidnapped and then rescued that the adrenaline crash was starting to slow him down. He looked a little more suspiciously around the street as he rushed to his family's apartment. Matt made it inside the door, locked it firmly behind him, and peered through the peephole to ensure that he wasn't followed. When he was satisfied, Matt exhaled and walked into the living room. LaBelle had made him paranoid.

"Oh, Matt!" Mrs. Brand came from the bedroom, holding her phone. "Dad called if you wanna say hi!"

Matt smiled and took the phone from his mom. "Hey, Pops!"

"Hey, Matt-Attack!" Matt's dad chuckled. "How's it going, bud?"

"Exhausting."

"Yeah? Mom said you were working overtime at the grocery store again?"

"Yeah, with all the chaos everywhere, we have people working ten- or twelve-hour shifts two or three days a week. Plus, we lost a couple of people in the produce team to Covid."

"Oh man, that sounds rough. I'm still in quarantine out here. Aunt Sue had me sleeping in the garage until last night cause she was worried I'd picked up something from the airport."

"Any idea when you'll be getting back?"

"Eh, they keep giving us vague, non-answers," Mr. Brand said and Matt could easily visualize the dismissive wave of his hand. "They say a few days, but that's gonna depend on what happens with my test results. A couple guys I know flew in late yesterday, so I'm hoping they'll let me fly out in the next day or two. I might be able to get to JFK and then take a car home or Mom can come pick me up."

"That sounds good," Matt nodded. "It'll be nice to have a sign that things are getting back to normal."

"Normal, huh? Looking to meet up with that girl you were talking to last night?"

"What?"

"Ah, you don't have to hide it from me," Matt's dad laughed. "Your mom said she heard you talking to her last night. Is she someone from your school?"

"She's, uh, from downtown. Really far downtown."

"Ah, is she cute?"

"Dad…"

"Alright, alright. Just wanted to ask. If you are interested, quarantine is a good time to lay down some groundwork, ya know?"

"If it turns out I need relationship advice, I'll come to you first."

"That's all I ask as a father. With all this overtime, have you been taking care of yourself?"

"Still showering, eating, and sleeping," Matt said.

"You gotta take care of more than your body, though. Gotta make sure you're still having fun. Get to do any new writing?"

"A little here and there," Matt said. "It's hard to keep motivated when it feels like time doesn't exist."

"Eh, something will come to you. You're a smart kid."

"Thanks," Matt said, looking at his mom gesturing for him to hand over the phone. "Mom wants to talk to you again."

"Before you go, one quick question: what's your new friend's name?"

"Goodnight, Dad," Matt said, passing the phone back over to his mom.

"Hello? I know, he's very cagey. Well, you were the one who wanted to do Good Cop, Bad Cop. I assumed I was going to be Good Cop!"

"You're both terrible," Matt laughed, heading into his bedroom. He closed the door behind him and took out his phone. After a few rings, Mira picked up on the other end.

"Hello?"

"Hey," Matt smiled. "I made it home, safe and sound."

"Good," Mira said, yawning. "Glad to hear it."

"Did I wake you?"

"A little, but I'm glad to know you're home. I'll let Dolly know you're safe, then I'll go to sleep. Thanks for sticking today out with me."

"Of course, I'll see you tomorrow."

"The Oak Hand didn't scare you away?"

"Not as bad as LaBelle scared them," Matt said. "Sleep well."

"Goodnight."

Matt hung up and slipped his phone into his pocket. He flopped onto his bed and rolled over to his notebook. He started writing down a bullet list of everything that had happened so far: meeting Mira, LaBelle, the diner, the Oak Hand, and everything else. The words flowed so easily and smoothly. Apparently, LaBelle could only take his voice, not his stories.

He'd seen so much, but LaBelle had stopped Matt from telling anyone about it with that magic bean. He thought he could trust his friends with what was going on or tell his parents enough to keep them from worrying. The Oak Hand, however, was a danger to everyone. After today, Matt wasn't sure if he could tell everyone the truth or if that would lead to more extremists. He could still write a truthful account but doubted anyone would believe it was real.

Mira of the Copper Tooth Clan, he wrote, *approached Matt Brand while he was stacking cans of soup on a beige, tin shelf with chipping paint.*

"You're doing it again."

LaBelle rolled his head to the left and saw Irene puttering around her terrarium. "Doing what?"

"That brooding thing you do when something isn't going your way. It's subtle, but it's different from your usual scowl."

"This is why I don't like roommates," LaBelle said. "We've been together less than fifty years and you already know my tells."

"I'm fae and you're easier to read than you think you are," Irene said, buzzing over and landing on LaBelle's bent knee. "What's up, boss?"

"Nothing," LaBelle said. "Just thinking."

"Need to talk?"

"You're my secretary. I don't pay you enough to be my therapist."

"Is it about Mira?"

"Yes."

"Is she in danger?"

LaBelle closed his eyes and leaned his head back over the couch. "I don't know."

"If she is—"

"She's probably not."

"But if she is," Irene stomped, barely registering on LaBelle's knee. "We need to help."

"Mira is perfectly safe now. I'm just frustrated. I had to kill five people today. They were from the Oak Hand, but it still feels like a waste. And Mira's case is muddled and confusing enough. Clues keep flicking in and out like a bulb with faulty wiring. I want to close this job and wash my hands of the whole thing."

"Blanc," Irene sighed. "I'm worried. I've never seen a case get to you like this."

"Mira's—it's complicated."

"How bad is it?"

LaBelle took a deep breath and leaned forward. "If it's what I think it is? It's not good."

Irene sighed. "You may not be fae, but you're very good at hiding the truth."

"If I told you before I was sure, I'm worried someone would ask you and get the wrong idea."

"It's that serious?"

LaBelle exhaled sharply and stood, startling the fairy off his knee. "I'm going to bed."

###

Mira couldn't sleep. She was exhausted, but preludes of nightmares kept her awake. Each time she closed her eyes and tried to settle, she was strangled by the feeling of the collar around her neck. After an hour of tossing and turning, Mira let out a frustrated grunt.

170

There was a knock that surprised her and Dolly opened the door slowly.

"Mira? You okay?"

"Yeah, sorry."

Dolly walked into the room and folded her legs underneath her so she was closer to Mira's eye level and propped her elbows on the mattress. "You don't have to be okay, if you're not."

"I just…" Mira struggled with the words as she sat up and pulled her knees to her chest. "Today didn't go how I planned."

"It's not your fault," Dolly said. "I know LaBelle was probably hard on you, but you don't have anything to feel guilty about."

"I was stupid."

"You were just excited," Dolly said, softly. "You had so many hopes about the Above and those were taken from you in an instant. That wasn't fair. You deserved a little happiness and it was stolen. But what they did to you? That doesn't mean you're dumb. It means they were cruel."

Mira nodded and picked at her fingernails. "Why did you come to the Above? After everything I've seen, I can't imagine why anyone would stay somewhere so dangerous."

"Well, there are a lot of Underfolk up here and no two have the same reasons," Dolly said. "My sister was kidnapped by the Oak Hand. She had snuck up briefly and they took her. When she didn't come back, I came up looking for her. I acted against the interest of my queen, defied an order from Viscount Valont, and went to find her.

I managed to save her from the Oak Hand, but I still defied the Fae Queen's command. To punish me, she banished me to the Above herself, cutting me off from my family and my home."

"She just cast you out? For rescuing your sister?"

"By going to the Above without permission, I doubled our chances of being discovered. I brought my sister back, but the Fae Queen wouldn't allow me to come home until she felt I had learned my lesson. It was difficult to adjust to the Above in my exile, but I was lucky enough to find LaBelle. He helped me get settled in with the Fold and even gave us the space for the diner and these rooms. I came hoping to find my sister, but I opened this place. I created a haven for people with nowhere to go."

"But why does anyone come up in the first place?" Mira asked. "LaBelle is connected with the Council so why would anyone want to come up here to see for themselves?"

"It's not quite the same," Dolly shook her head. "It's less about information. The Fae Queen has a long history of stealing humans away and bringing them down to the Under. The magi pass easily for humans and come up in droves to learn about technology, culture, and things that they can't experience otherwise. And the beasts that chose to stay in the Above are explorers or looking for a new place to call home. Besides, there's more to the Above than the comings and goings of humans."

"What do you mean?"

"My sister, for example, came to the Above because she wanted to run in the rain. The Under is safe, but some Underfolk are too wild to stay underground forever. Dragons still live in their remote caves and herds of wild centaurs exist in places too remote for humans, but living away from them limits our magic. It's a hard decision to make, but I know fae folk who would give up all their magic to fly on a fresh breeze or run in the rain. Some people come up for new knowledge, but some of us come up to remember what we used to be."

"I guess so," Mira said, thinking about the first time she'd gotten a chance to look at the sky. "I just can't believe my mom would ever—with one of those people!"

"She didn't, though." Dolly put a hand on Mira's arm. "Whoever she found up here? He wasn't like the Oak Hand. Those kinds of people? They don't just hate when they see us. They hate all the time and I know Underfolk who hate humans just as passionately."

"I don't know how she could ever see the good in any of them."

"You see the good in Matt."

"That's different."

"Is it?" Dolly smirked. "You've been up here for two days and he's your best friend, isn't he? How is that different from anything your mother might have done?"

"I don't know. Matt's different."

"And I'm sure there are lots of other humans like Matt. The problem is that hate is loud. You have to listen for love."

Mira frowned and wrung her hands together. Dolly lifted Mira's chin to meet her eyes with a kind smile. "Is that all that's bothering you?"

"It's too quiet," Mira said. "I like having all this space to myself, but I guess I miss the familiarity of being close to my clan. And I keep closing my eyes and it feels like I'm alone in that room again with that collar around my neck and I—"

"Hey, hey," Dolly shook Mira's arm gently. "Take a deep breath. You're here and I'm with you. You're safe."

Mira nodded and took a slow breath. She sniffled a little and rubbed her face with the back of her hand.

"I got an idea," Dolly said, cheerfully. "Wait here."

Dolly heaved herself off the floor and slowly clomped down the hall. Mira waited a minute, hugging her knees to her chest. Before long, she heard hooves coming back and perked up. Dolly returned with a large, pink conch shell in her hands.

"I've seen my fair share of magical artifacts," Dolly said. "And I'm a bit of a packrat when I see something I like. The lost and found is fair game after a month and I'd rather grow my collection than throw things away."

"A shell?"

"It's a simple incantation," Dolly said. "Even a first-year student at the University of Fire could cast it, but that doesn't make it any less soothing."

Mira took the shell and turned it in her hands. There was a quiet hissing coming from the opening and she raised the conch to her ear. The sound of rushing water came from deep in the spiral, the steady tempo of waves crashing against an invisible shore. "It sounds like the ocean!"

"I thought you'd enjoy that part of your day," Dolly smiled. "Now, instead of ending up in that room, you'll be on the waterfront again."

"Thanks," Mira said, holding the shell close to her chest. "It really means a lot."

"Now," Dolly hugged Mira tightly. "Get some sleep. And if you need anything else? I'm just down the hall."

"Thanks. Goodnight."

Mira settled into bed as Dolly closed the door behind her. She set the big shell on the table by her side and focused on the sound of the waves. She pulled the blanket up over her shoulders and snuggled up against the soft mattress, smoothing out her ponytail and closing her eyes.

For a brief moment, she was back in the Oak Hand's lair, struggling to breathe with the metal collar around her neck. She kept her eyes closed and focused on the sounds of the waves coming from the pink shell. Mira could taste the salt in the air as she imagined the sea spray. She wasn't in the warehouse anymore. Mira was on the pier with Matt and she was sad, but she was alive and she felt safe wrapped in his arm. Mira counted the waves crashing and drifted off to sleep, listening to the sounds of the ocean.

Chapter 16

Matt woke up the next morning with his face stuck to the notebook he'd spent the night writing in. He wasn't sure what time he'd fallen asleep, but his narrative ended around the point when he and Mira were in the diner for the first time. Wiping the drool off his chin, Matt closed the notebook and checked the clock. If he were still at the grocery store, he'd be running late. Matt got ready to head to the diner, but his mom was sitting with her cup of coffee in the kitchen.

"Hey, Matt," she smiled, looking at the clock. "I thought you had the early shift today?"

"Uh, they said I could come in late today because I worked a longer shift yesterday."

"Oh," Matt's mom shrugged. "Well, have a good day. Be safe."

"I will!" Matt said, rushing out the door. He'd tell his mom that he'd been fired as soon as everything with Mira was resolved. The mission was more important than minimum wage.

Driving through downtown, Matt couldn't help but watch for large vans following behind him, but the roads were abandoned without so much as a bicycle trailing him. The diner wasn't flanked by men in windbreakers and Matt finally felt that he was safe in his town again.

The breakfast shift had ended and the diner was nearly empty except for the staff. Dolly was wiping down menus at the counter and Daryl came waddling out with pots and pans in the kitchen. Mira sat at the counter with her hair tied back in a sleek ponytail, eating a waffle with strawberries.

"Matt!" Dolly grinned. "I hope you're hungry. Mira made corn muffins this morning and she made sure to save you one."

"You keep giving that stray dog scraps," the dwarf grumbled from the kitchen, "and people are gonna wonder why they pay at all!"

"They're Mira's muffins!" Dolly snapped back, pulling a corn muffin out of the baking cabinet and serving it on a plate. "She wants to be generous with them and I won't stop her."

"Thanks, Dolly," Matt said. He sat next to Mira and smiled at her. "You okay?"

"Yeah," Mira smiled, putting her fork and knife aside. "I really think I am."

"LaBelle!" Dolly smiled as the detective came in. "Eatin' on the run or do you want one of Mira's famous muffins with your breakfast?"

"Don't put my eggs on the griddle yet, Dolly," LaBelle said, taking off his hat. "I'm just stopping in before hitting the street."

LaBelle sat at the counter on Mira's other side and smiled. "I'm heading down into the Under today. I plan to talk to the Sphinxes and maybe your teacher. With what I know so far, I should have this resolved by the end of the day."

"You think so?" Mira asked, hopeful.

"I'd bet money on it," LaBelle affirmed. "What's your tutor's name?"

"Ezeel," Mira said. "They're a scholar at the University of Fire."

"Got it," LaBelle tapped his temple twice.

"What happens when you find out who we're looking for?" Matt asked, picking at his muffin.

"We go talk to Mira's father. Once I get a few more details, I can cast a locating spell and we should be able to have this all resolved by dinner. Now, stay here and stay safe, please?" LaBelle asked. Mira nodded and LaBelle started towards the door. "Dolly? Keep a stool open for me at dinner."

"Will do," Dolly said. Once LaBelle was gone, Dolly nearly galloped over towards Mira and clapped her hands. "Oh, this will be wonderful! Are you excited?"

"Excited," Mira nodded, talking a mile a minute, "and nauseous and scared and a whole bunch of other emotions that I can't describe. I should go pack! I need a suitcase—wait, where can I get a suitcase? Dolly, I need a plastic bag!"

"Mira," Dolly laughed, "slow down. As far as packing goes, I got an old backpack you can use. Consider anything you can carry in that room yours…even accounting for troll strength."

"Thanks, Dolly," Mira said. She took a deep breath and put her hands flat on the counter. "I just don't know what to do with all this energy."

"Try using it to go pick out what you want to bring home," Dolly said, pointing upstairs. "Anything you need, let me know."

"Thanks, Dolly. Matt, wanna come up for a bit?"

"Sure," Matt smiled and followed Mira up to her room. There was a big, spiral shell on Mira's bedside table that made noises like the ocean. Mira started going through all her bureau and put some t-shirts and a pair of jeans on her mattress. She added the contents of each drawer onto the modest pile of belongings, topping it off with the shell and her raincoat.

"I can't believe it's finally gonna happen!" Mira said, folding and refolding the clothing. "I've been waiting for years to meet my dad and now that he's so close? I'm just…tingling with excitement! Maybe I could go to school, too! I mean, there's a lot to catch up on, but I have the option! Last weekend, my life felt like it was over, but now there are so many possibilities!"

"I'm happy for you," Matt smiled, sitting on the bed. "It's great to see you getting everything you wanted."

"And if you hadn't taken a chance with me, I might still be hiding between the chips and soda."

"You would have found a way, but I'm glad I got to see you through to the end."

"And we can still be friends!" Mira took Matt's hands. "We can hang out here at the diner and explore Hedgefield. We can ride an elevator!"

Matt laughed and nodded. "I'm glad you finally get the family you wanted."

Mira sat closer to Matt and put her arms around him in a tight hug. "I feel like home is somewhere up here, but you were my family first."

###

Today, the party in Fae Town was more subdued, but the fae folk still drew magic from the air to conjure festive fireworks and twinkling lights. A pair of water nymphs skated across the surface of a fountain, chased by a young satyr who fell face first into the water in his pursuit. LaBelle didn't have time to stop today. Slipping from shadow to shadow, LaBelle managed to avoid any fae from seeing him. He didn't have the energy to plaster on a fake smile to refuse a glass of fae wine. Shadow Walking wasn't magical, but it was all he needed to get out of Fae Town.

Walking into Brodal, LaBelle strode confidently through the bustling city center, only noticing the city in his periphery. An elf argued with a dwarf in the classic debate of rune work against enchantment. A vampire was handing over a few precious stones to a necromancer's skeletal assistant in exchange for a bottle of blood. An oracle sat on the side of the road, sifting through her tarot deck. They all gave LaBelle a wide berth as he marched to the University of Fire.

"LaBelle!"

LaBelle turned and dropped his shoulders as an annoyed sorceress rushed toward him with the fury of a hurricane behind her. "Aili," LaBelle started to walk away, "I'm afraid I don't have time for—"

"You used magic against humans?" Aili snapped. "Five dead and a burned down warehouse? For the River's sake, you summoned lightning in broad daylight! Do you have any idea how much work it will take for me to cover this up?"

"I think you've handled worse."

"LaBelle!" Aili grabbed his wrist, pulling him away from the busy street and into an alleyway. "You can't just go around killing anyone you like!"

"They were Oak Hand," LaBelle snarled, starting to lose his temper. "If you were in my shoes—"

"I'm not saying I'd want to be in your position. The Magi Prima has always had a firm stance against the Oak Hand, but we've maintained a distance from them since—"

"If Mira was a witch or a sorceress, would we be having this conversation? If she were a magi would you be this angry?"

"I'm sorry that she got in over her head," Aili said, swallowing her anger. "I just wish this could have been handled without killing half a dozen people in the process. This will not be an easy fix."

"Well, I'm sorry for the inconvenience." LaBelle pulled free of Aili's grip with a scowl. "I'll fill out the paperwork next time."

"Blanc," Aili said, firmly, "what's gotten into you? Is this about your case?"

"It's—I did what was necessary. I'm sorry for making trouble for you."

"You know who her father is, don't you? And something about it scares you."

LaBelle sighed and leaned against the wall behind him. "Her father is blinded in the Fae's vision. Mira and Matt consulted a mermaid to find him, but his face was blocked."

"The number of humans in the Above blocked from the sight of the Fae is small," Aili said. "So, what's the problem? Shouldn't you be happy to be finished with the case?"

"The problem is that I'm wondering why her mother wouldn't tell anyone. I don't know why she kept it a secret from the night she got back until the day she died. It wasn't shame or she would have treated Mira horribly. It wasn't honor or she would have hailed the name of the child's father to her clan."

"Then what's left?"

"What if her father was someone so dangerous and powerful that she was afraid? What if she was scared that whoever Mira's father was —?"

"Is half of Mira's bloodline," Aili finished. "And you think she's truly something evil?"

"Mira? No, I don't think so," LaBelle shook his head. "Her father? Well, let's just hope I'm wrong."

"I hear you struck a deal with Dural to get you until the end of the day."

"I'd ask for an extension, but I fear that her kidnapping won't be a very convincing argument."

Aili nodded. "Tread carefully, Blanc. Whoever Mira's father is, it's not someone that should be toyed with. They're powerful enough to hide from a fae's vision—whether that's for good or ill, I wouldn't push your luck."

"Believe me, if I'm right? Luck has nothing to do with it."

"Whatever you need to do to resolve this issue," Aili said, cautious, "no one would blame you. You could walk away right now, pretend you didn't find anything, and bring Mira back to her clan."

"I can't," LaBelle said. "It's not about pride or my need to have all my questions answered. I owe Mira something after all this. She just lost her mother, she deserves closure…the chance at happiness if nothing else."

"I hope she gets that much."

"Hell, I could be wrong," LaBelle chuckled, trying to reassure the sorceress. "I've been around long enough to make lots of mistakes. This whole 'Fae Queen Favor' thing could be a dead end."

"Perhaps," Aili said. "I trust you to make the right choice for everyone involved: Mira, her father, the Under, everyone."

"I'll be sure to keep the Council informed when I have the final answer. I'm sure you all want that as much as I do."

"So, what are you waiting for?"

"I need to be prepared," LaBelle said, walking down the alley towards the busy street. "Just in case I'm right."

<u>Chapter 17</u>

Academic pursuits were popular among the magi, but career scholars resided in the University of Fire under the shadow of the Victory Tower. LaBelle overheard the conversations of spell-crafters as he walked through the courtyard: debates on the superior methods of commanding elements, discussions about the most recent research on abjuration spells to protect against hazardous mercury, and an all-out argument about which conjuration rune in a circle summoned a flock of angry crows rather than the stag the casters intended. LaBelle found it funny that after ages of being wrong, people still always hoped it was someone else's fault before trying to resolve the problem.

Walking through the halls of the University of Fire, LaBelle could smell the alchemical substances burning, herbs being crushed, and smoke from a thousand failed spells that fizzled out. The air hummed with magic energy freshly discharged from wands and LaBelle felt like he was trekking through a heavy rainstorm about to roar with thunder. He walked through the halls until he found an office with a brass nameplate on the door: *Professor Ezeel, Mundane Arts.*

LaBelle loitered by the office door for a minute and waited. Ezeel was a tall, thin elf with pointed ears as long as LaBelle's middle finger. Their ears were studded with brass rings and chains, prominently glittering against their shaved black head. The professor's office was about the size of LaBelle's bedroom, though cramped with full bookshelves, stacks of loose volumes on the floor, and a large chair for Ezeel to sit opposite their students. Ezeel was flipping through a magazine while sipping a cup of something minty and steaming. LaBelle knocked on the door frame and Ezeel looked up from their reading. "Can I help you?"

"Professor Ezeel? I'm wondering if you have a moment to talk."

"I suppose." Ezeel closed the magazine and stood to meet LaBelle's eye. "Though I don't see how I could be of interest to Blanc LaBelle."

"Have we met?"

"No, but the professor I share a classroom with teaches Arcane and Above History. It's hard not to hear your name once or twice a week. Just yesterday I overheard the tail end of a discussion about your artistic foray in the Renaissance. For an immortal, you're not very good at blending in."

"I'd rather be forgotten where it counts. Do you have a moment to talk about a student?"

"I'm afraid I can't discuss student's grades," Ezeel explained, moving to a bookcase and trying to shelve a loose volume into one of the few gaps. "But if you're looking to discuss their character—"

"Her grades aren't my concern at the moment," LaBelle interrupted, stepping into the professor's office. "Do you remember Mira of the Copper Tooth Clan?"

"I see very few trolls come through these halls," Ezeel said, fondly, "but I've only ever seen one half-troll. She was a sweet girl, Mira. Smart…brilliant, even. If half the wizards who came to my class were as eager to learn Mundane Arts as she was, I'd have a bigger office."

"She was a good student?"

"I was hesitant," Ezeel said, returning to their chair, "but I was all too happy to be proven wrong. With a few diction lessons, she was speaking as clearly as someone without tusks. She could write clearly and well. I couldn't give her enough to read!"

"She said you let her read magic instruction?"

"Only for practice. Nothing too advanced, but enough that she had to pay attention to understand it all."

"How did she become your student?" LaBelle asked, looking at the bookshelves. Volumes of ancient history and antique scrolls were interspersed with paperback novels and language learning books.

"Her mother approached me," Ezeel said. "I have a reputation for teaching young trolls how to pass for human beyond the mask of a glamour: behavior, speech, manners, all the things you can't hide with illusion. I'd taught Mira's mother enough for her own explorations of the Above. If it had been anyone else, I might not have taken Mira on as a student. But you must know how Kaysar is when she gets something in her head."

"Can't say I've had the pleasure."

"Oh?"

"Kaysar's dead."

"Since when?"

"Last week. Calcite disease."

Ezeel slumped in their chair and dropped their arms down to their side. They looked away and put a hand over their mouth. Elf grief was difficult to spot, but LaBelle figured this was as close as the professor would get to weeping. "Shame," they whispered. "She was a good friend."

"Why did she want Mira to study with you? Did she want Mira to explore the Above as well?"

"I suppose, she wanted Mira to have every opportunity. I think part of Kaysar knew Mira would be happier in the Above. Part of Mira belongs to that world and I hope that she has the opportunity to be where she belongs. I didn't think I'd like tutoring a half-troll, but Mira was one of my favorite students."

"Favorite enough to adopt?"

"What about her father?"

"I'm exploring all options," LaBelle said. "If she asked, would you adopt Mira?"

"Are you familiar with troll adoption rites?"

"I've seen it once or twice."

"The only way for me to adopt her is to fight one of her clan members," Ezeel said, going back to moving a pile of books on the floor to a shelf. "And troll fights are usually to the death."

"You might win."

Ezeel let out a short, sharp laugh like a cough. "You have more faith in my abilities than I do."

"You're a professor at the University of Fire and—"

"I'm an English tutor!" Ezeel scoffed. "I'm not a warrior! I like Mira, but my dying is of no possible help to her. Bring her to her father."

"Do you know who her father is? It seems like a family secret that died with Kaysar."

"I couldn't tell you if I knew," Ezeel said. They settled and leaned against the back of their chair. "LaBelle, if Kaysar never told Mira about her father, why would she tell me? Besides, Kaysar must have had a reason to keep it secret. Did it occur to you that there's a reason Mira doesn't know who her father is? If Kaysar never told Mira, why should you stick your nose in it?"

"Mira came to me asking for her father because she doesn't have her mother to protect her. If I can't find him or some other solution, she'll be going back to the troll clans. She doesn't want that."

"I'm sorry," Ezeel sighed, "but I'm no savior. She might have to just tolerate the trolls for another two years."

"She might not survive there without her mother."

"Then I hope her father accepts her," Ezeel said, frowning. "Is there anything else I can help you with today?"

"I suppose not," LaBelle said. "Unless I could ask for a favor."

"If you bear in mind that I'm a coward, you're welcome to anything I can offer."

"Can I have this?" LaBelle asked, picking up the magazine from Ezeel's chair. "It would save me the trouble of going back up to the Above."

"That?" Ezeel shrugged. "Certainly. It's just a Hollywood gossip magazine. It's a guilty pleasure I grabbed the last time I visited the Above. Why the interest?"

"I'm hoping it'll be enough to catch the interest of a sphinx."

###

The sphinxes lived on the opposite side of the Under City, but LaBelle felt more comfortable taking the long walk around the Brodal ring than taking unnecessary risks in the domain of the beasts. It would take less time to go through Fae Town, but LaBelle worried he'd be swept up into some kind of endless party and he wasn't in the mood to celebrate.

LaBelle focused on the case as he walked through the magi city, ignoring the shopkeepers and restauranteurs trying to entice him into their establishments. While he felt he'd reach the end of the trail, he didn't want to go back to Mira until he was sure. He knew he was looking for something to prove him wrong. As he crossed into the threshold of the Outerlands, LaBelle knew that any last chance to be wrong would be kept in the careful possession of the sphinxes.

Unlike the Victory Tower of Brodal, the Sphinx's Temple was meant to scare people away. Jagged towers of gray stone threatened to fall and crash onto intruders if they stepped on the wrong place. The entryway had sets of sharp stalactites hanging down, like a gaping maw ready to bite down on anyone who dared walk up the tattered, wine-red carpet that led to the domain of the sphinxes. As opposed to the welcoming halls of academia that LaBelle had just come from, the Sphinx's Temple was a foreboding tomb of mystery and secrets.

LaBelle walked up the steps and waited at the mouth of the stone fortress. Books were packed tightly into the shelves with scrolls filling every inch of every space with little regard for traditional organization. The sphinxes cared little for traditional treasure, but knowledge— secrets, in particular—was of great value to them, no matter what the subject. The light from outside the sphinx's lair ended in a perfectly round arc a few paces from the temple's entrance and LaBelle stayed just at the edge of that perimeter. A slight breeze came from the back of the library, carrying the scent of musty paper and old ink mixed with the decay of an unfortunate trespasser who lacked LaBelle's manners. In the small curve of light, two high tables came up to LaBelle's elbow, but there was nowhere to sit. This was not a place to loiter.

LaBelle didn't flinch when he heard a low growl over his left shoulder. Turning slowly, he looked up to see a pair of broad, feline paws perched on top of one of the shelves. White wings unfolded and the lion's body pounced down, gliding a little to guide her descent to land right in front of LaBelle. The woman's face had bright green eyes, an unruly gray mane, and sharp teeth that grinned hungrily at him. The sphinx blinked as she slowly circled, sniffing him. LaBelle stood his ground, keeping to the rules of the Outerlands.

"Always smiles or maybe frowns," the sphinx sneered as she prowled, her voice low and husky, "sinks in water, never drowns. Catches prey with its barbed teeth, hunts all day but never eats. What am I?"

"A fishhook," LaBelle replied, confidently.

The sphinx grinned and relaxed, sitting on her haunches to look at LaBelle. "And what do you seek, LaBelle?"

"I want to know the names of anyone the Fae Queen has hidden from those looking in the Veil and a list of any troll with access to a glamour, both within the last twenty years or so."

"Specific information," the sphinx said, showing her sharp teeth, "but it can be found. Do you make an offer for my knowledge?"

"I offer secrets from the Above," LaBelle said, lifting the magazine. "Truths once hidden by those who stand in the light of celebrity."

The sphinx snatched the tabloid from LaBelle's hand and swatted it onto the stone floor, spreading it open. She flipped through the pages awkwardly with her flat paws but reveled in the words. "Mmmm… affairs, facades, and shames of the famous," the sphinx purred. "I do so love to see their truths laid bare."

"Then you'll find what I ask for?"

The sphinx blinked her glowing eyes slowly and closed the magazine, leaving her payment until LaBelle's request was fulfilled. "Wait here…"

Unfolding her wings, the sphinx pushed off the ground and banked over the shelves. LaBelle leaned on one of the tables and followed her movements by listening to the feathery wings, the creak of wooden shelves, and the rustling of paper. He could have gone looking for the information, but without the sphinx's help, he'd be lost in the deep labyrinth of shelves that hid eons of wisdom from prying eyes. Some people would die before getting out of the maze, but most would be eaten by the sphinxes lurking in the stacks. In LaBelle's case, he couldn't afford to waste the time.

Wingbeats alerted LaBelle that the sphinx was returning and he straightened. The creature landed on the stone floor and deposited a scroll of fresh parchment and a thick, leather book on one of the high tables. The sphinx took a few steps back and sat with her magazine so that LaBelle could peruse the items in some semblance of peace. LaBelle nodded his thanks and looked at the scroll first.

The Fae Queen hadn't added many new names to her list of favored in the last hundred years, but LaBelle read them all carefully. He recognized a lot of the names of inventors, artists, builders, and other creators the Fae Queen admired. He also recognized criminals guilty of destruction, suffering, and pain to such an unimaginable degree that they were erased from history after their death. There were some names he knew too well, a few humans that LaBelle had helped put away, and a few he had liked. The list was shorter when LaBelle considered who was likely dead. Carefully, LaBelle rolled up the scroll and tapped his thumb against the table as he thought about the most likely candidates on the list. He'd hoped the list would inspire him to consider someone else as Mira's father, but the scroll only confirmed his suspicions so far.

LaBelle opened the book, a running registry of manufactured glamours. Glamours weren't uncommon but they were closely monitored by the magi bureaucrats. Each one was registered to an individual with a description of how the glamour made them appear and why they wanted it. Most of the entries were connected to magi, followed by fae as the second most popular. Kaysar was the only troll that had a glamour in the last thirty years.

"This is it?" LaBelle asked. "So few trolls with glamours?"

"Trolls have never had much interest in the Above," the sphinx said, flipping through the tabloid. "And there are few who care to meddle with magic."

"If I was looking for someone else—"

"The sphinxes pride our collection on accuracy," the sphinx said, closing her magazine. "If you don't like the answers, I can't change facts for your comfort."

"This can't be right!" LaBelle snapped, slamming the book shut. "There has to be something that we don't know. The Fae Queen doesn't know about someone who's blocked, an unregistered glamour, anything that would make sense!"

"Unwelcome, difficult, precious, and rare," the sphinx grinned, collecting the materials off the table. "Once it's revealed, sits heavy in the air. What am I?"

Cackling, the sphinx pumped her wings and flew into the darkness of the library before LaBelle could snap at her. He dropped his shoulders and shook his head. "The truth," LaBelle answered, quieter. "Damn it, I hate being right."

<u>Chapter 18</u>

Mira had struggled to get through the lunch shift. She didn't have much to do in the kitchen beyond dishes and kept stopping in the middle of scrubbing pans when she started to daydream. After the lunch rush, Dolly let her come out and bundle silverware at the counter so she could talk to Matt. She was grateful to have something to do with her hands, but her leg was bouncing every time she looked down.

"And once the quarantine is lifted," Matt continued making plans with Mira, "we can go to the pier when the rides are open and we can go up on the Ferris Wheel. We can go to a movie together and—"

"What about elevators? My mother always told me about elevators!"

"We'll ride every one in the city!"

"This is so exciting!" Dolly came out and put a hand on Mira's shoulder. "I'm nervous and it's not even my dad!"

"Can I keep working at the diner?" Mira asked. "Even if I'm not living upstairs?"

"If you do, we'll be able to pay you!" Dolly said. "I wouldn't dream of letting you go that easy! And you can bring your dad around so we can all get to know him."

"Inviting humans into the diner?" Matt asked. "That's a sign of change."

"We let you stick around," Dolly winked. "And you're human."

"How did you know?"

"You gotta be pretty quick to get past me. I've had my suspicions since you first came in. Mira let it slip last night by accident. I almost didn't notice, but there were a few dead giveaways when I look back on it. I mean, even the grandson of a magi knows if he wants a shot of Witch Hazel in his milkshake!"

"We're sorry we lied," Mira frowned, "but LaBelle—"

"LaBelle can be paranoid," Dolly said. "Rightly so, of course. He's met enough humans to have his fair share of disappointments about them, but I'm fae. I have to trust that there's good in people."

"Still, we should have told you," Matt said.

"You've been a good friend to Mira," Dolly beamed. "And I'd rather invite a good human than the worst kind of Underfolk into my place. It'll take some getting used to, but you can stop by whenever you like. And if anyone harasses you, they'll answer to my back hoof!"

"I never took you for the violent type," Mira laughed.

"Only with the people I care about. Besides, if your father starts coming around, it'd be nice if Matt helps soften the blow with a human's perspective. He's only been here a few days, but he's had more positive experiences than a lot of humans have with Underfolk in a lifetime."

The old payphone on the wall started ringing. Dolly furrowed her brow and trotted over to answer it. "Hello?" Dolly paused and rolled her eyes. "LaBelle, why can't you call my cell like a normal person? Ugh, never mind. Sure thing. Mira! It's for you."

Mira's heart leaped to her chest, threatening to fly away with the rest of her body. She smiled, dropped the silverware back into their respective bins, and rushed over to the phone, nearly slipping on the tile floor in her urgency. Dolly giggled a little and handed Mira the phone, waiting excitedly.

"Hello?" Mira asked.

"Mira, hey, how's it going?" LaBelle asked.

"Fine. Did you get the information you needed?"

"Yeah. It was all there."

"You don't sound very excited," Mira's heart dropped. It felt like there was a stone working its way down her throat and into her stomach.

"Mira…" LaBelle struggled with the words. "We should have this conversation face-to-face. Can you meet me outside in a few minutes?"

"Did you find my dad or not?" Mira tightened her grip on the phone as her confusion turned to anxiety and fear. The sinking feeling had made its way to her lungs and weighed her entire body down. She could already feel her heart breaking.

"I'm sorry, Mira," LaBelle sighed. "I didn't promise you'd like what I found."

Matt slowed his car as LaBelle raised his wand, moving it in a quick sigil to unlock the gate to Rook Hill Cemetery. The metal fence squealed open and Matt pulled his car through. He drove up the paved path, taking extra care not to disturb any of the headstones close to the road.

"This one here," LaBelle pointed. "Third one—Mira, wait!"

Mira threw open the door and raced down the row of headstones. Matt frantically put the car in park and followed as fast as he could while LaBelle calmly brought up the rear at a slow walk. Mira stopped running through the graves and fell to her knees. Tears were slipping down her face, staining her mask with dark streaks under her eyes. She slumped over, clutching her stomach and sucking in shaky breaths.

"Mira?" Matt reached out to touch her, but Mira slapped his hand away.

"Give her some space," LaBelle warned, leading Matt back a few paces. "Just let her—"

Mira tore her mask off, threw her head back, and yelled. The scream was loud and echoed over the graves, scaring birds out of the surrounding trees. When she was out of breath, Mira gripped her stomach again and doubled over, pressing her forehead into the grass. She wept into the ground and her whole body shook with the sobs.

Matt's heart broke seeing her this hurt. He knew that Mira wasn't just crying because of a father she never knew. She'd lost her chance at life in the Above, a place that she'd started to call home. She'd lost her chance to have a family. Matt had lost grandparents and even a great aunt, but he could always go back to his family. Mira's heartbreak was heavier because she didn't have anything to go back to. It was the kind of loss Matt could feel in his bones, not just his heart.

"Let's give her a minute," LaBelle whispered, nudging Matt's shoulder. "She needs some time to grieve alone. It's a troll thing."

Matt was reluctant to go but eventually followed LaBelle back to the car. The detective leaned on the hood by the right wheel well, keeping a wary eye on Mira as Matt leaned on the passenger side door. "Who was he?"

"Does it matter?" LaBelle asked, coldly.

"It might matter to Mira."

LaBelle let out a long breath but nodded. "He was favored by the Fae Queen. A musician by night who spent his days scratching lyrics on the back of napkins at the restaurant he bartended at. He and Mira's mom had a fling on one of her expeditions."

"That's all there is?"

"What do you want, a biography?" LaBelle snarled, annoyed. "He died in a car crash three years ago. No other family, but some friends pitched in to bury him."

"Could we take Mira to one of those friends?"

"It doesn't work like that. Whoever we bring Mira to needs to have a direct blood relation to her. Even taking her to her father was a long shot."

Matt kicked a stone. "I feel like we got robbed."

"You're only sixteen, right? The fact is that life isn't fair. It doesn't care if you do everything right. You can follow every rule someone gives you, but life might still sneak up and sucker punch you."

"It doesn't feel right. There has to be some way she can stay."

"The only other way is if someone adopts her."

"Great! Maybe I can talk my parents into—"

"Troll adoption is resolved by combat," LaBelle said. "It's for the protection of the child as much as the clan. Anyone from outside her clan who wants to adopt Mira has to beat a member of her clan in a fight."

"So, we'd have to literally fight for her freedom?"

"She's going home, not to prison."

"She clearly doesn't want to be there!" Matt snapped and turned to LaBelle. "Why do we have to follow all these stupid rules?"

"Because if we don't follow these stupid rules," LaBelle said, calmly, "the very delicate balance of the Under would be upturned. Imagine Mira's clan coming up from the Under to find her. Then another clan will come up to try and compete for what they see as contested territory. They'll go into war over Hedgefield. Next thing you know, the goblins want a piece of the action. Then the harpies, the dragons, and every other monster from fairytales come up. Then the magi and the fae arrive to restore balance, of course. Next thing you know, it's an all-out war for the Above."

"Just because we don't make Mira go back to the Under?"

"Very delicate," LaBelle repeated. He looked away and Matt followed his gaze to Mira. "You can go to her now, if you want. Just be careful."

Matt stood and walked down the rows of graves towards Mira. She was sitting on the grass with her legs underneath her, staring at the headstone as tears rolled down her face. Matt sat down next to her and looked at the grave. Any words of comfort felt hollow, so he said the only thing he knew was true. "I'm sorry."

"Everything I worked for," Mira shook her head. "I risked everything to do this and nothing changed."

"Hey, it wasn't nothing. At least you know."

"I almost wish I didn't know." Mira wiped her eyes. "I'm sorry we won't get to ride the elevator together."

"You don't have to be sorry."

"I should feel sad," Mira said, "but I don't. I'm just angry at him for not helping me. That sounds so selfish, but I wish he could just be here for me now."

"That's allowed," Matt said. "There's no right way to feel something like this. Emotions are never wrong. And you have a right to be angry with him."

"Then why aren't I angry with my mom?" Mira asked. "She isn't here when I need her either."

"Grief is…" Matt frowned, trying to find comforting words. "It's a very human thing. You can feel whatever you want or you can feel nothing. Maybe things would be better if we all felt bad when someone died, but we don't. When we lose those we feel close to, we feel sad about. But those who we wanted to help us, we just feel angry."

Mira wiped her eyes again and shifted so she was sitting cross-legged in front of the grave. "I'd hoped I could grieve more like a human."

"Would you like to?" Matt asked. "I didn't know him well, but—"

"I wanna sit for a minute," Mira said, ripping up a handful of grass.

"Do you want to be alone?"

Mira sniffled and shook her head. "I've got a whole lifetime of being alone and I'd rather not be on my own during this."

Matt folded his legs, patiently waiting with Mira while she grieved in the cemetery. He looked back at LaBelle, still leaning against the hood of Matt's car with his arms folded. Bowing his head, Matt put his hands on the grass and waited. The birds started to come back to a nearby tree and a few high branches scraped against each other in the breeze. Cars passed behind them on the main road, but Matt felt like the rest of the world was grieving with them. Mira reached out for more grass, but gently touched Matt's hand instead. Matt turned his hand to fit her palm and squeezed her fingers.

Finally, Mira took a deep breath and sighed, dropping her shoulders. "This sucks."

"Yeah. It really does."

"I think I'm ready to go now."

"Are you sure?"

"It's not like sitting here will change anything." Mira shrugged, stood up, and brushed her jeans off. Matt stood with her and wiped his hands clean. She took a few steps closer to the grave, knelt by it, rested her forehead on the stone, and closed her eyes.

"I don't know if you can hear me," Mira whispered, just loud enough for Matt to hear, "but I hope you found peace. I hope that you are in the Hall of your Forbearers and that you will see my mother again. Kaysar waited for you. Her whole life long, she never married or took another to her bed. She loved you. I hope you knew that."

Mira stood again and looked down at the grave. "I accepted what has happened, but I do not forgive you."

Pulling her mask back on, Mira turned and started slowly walking back to the car with Matt. "I'm sorry," she said. "If I knew this was the end of the road, I wouldn't have wasted your time."

"Mira," Matt smiled, taking her hand, "I've had more adventure in the past few days than the rest of my life. And now I know there's all these Underfolk and the diner and trolls and…others like you. There's a lot of good people in the Under and maybe I can help them, too."

"I hope you're right," Mira said. "You're a good friend, probably my best friend. But don't tell Dolly? She might get jealous."

"I feel like she knows," Matt smiled and squeezed Mira's hand a little. As they got closer to the car, LaBelle straightened but kept his eyes forward. Mira stopped walking, hesitating in front of the backdoor to look at him.

"I'm sorry, Mira," LaBelle said.

"It doesn't feel like you are," Mira snarled. She opened the back door, slid in, and slammed the door before LaBelle could respond. Without another word, LaBelle got in before Matt had fully rounded the car.

Matt had to do a quick double-take. LaBelle was looking down and away from the car as he opened his door, but Matt could swear that he'd seen the detective's lips tighten. His face sagged a little and he hunched into himself as he buckled in. LaBelle hardly seemed the type to let a girl's words cut him so deeply and he didn't seem the sort to be upset about the death of someone he didn't know. Unnerved,

Matt walked around the front of the car and climbed into the joyless vehicle.

Chapter 19

"But I can't go back to the caves!" Mira pleaded. "If I go back there, the trolls will—!"

"Mira, this isn't a debate!" LaBelle said. "Your bloodline is still tied to your clan. I have to respect that law."

"They'll kill me, LaBelle!" Mira yelled. "Or they might as well! Mayza might pity me and let me sleep by her doorstep, but without a family to claim me, I'm at the whims of the clan! I might survive, but it won't be a life worth living!"

Dolly had closed up the diner early in the hope of good news, but Mira had come in and cried in Dolly's arms for a solid minute before LaBelle told her to go pack. Mira needed to be back in the troll caves before sundown.

"Just until you're eighteen," LaBelle said, "then you'll be independent and—"

"This is so unfair!" Mira said. "If I go back, I'm doomed! I'll get scraps of other people's meals and I won't have any property because everything I have will belong to the clan!"

"Mira, this isn't my choice to make! If it helps, I can come down with you and—"

"And what?" Mira scoffed. "Tell the Copper Tooth clan to be nicer to me? If you think that'll work, you're as delusional as you are cruel!"

Mira stood up from the table and ran to her room upstairs. Matt followed after her, their feet stomping up the steps in tandem. LaBelle leaned back and closed his eyes as a door slammed upstairs. When he opened them, Dolly was staring down at him with Irene on her shoulder, equally mad.

"What?" LaBelle asked, raising his hands.

"She's right and you know it," Irene grumbled.

"If anyone has a better solution," LaBelle said, "I'd welcome it!"

"She's just one troll!" Dolly snapped. "Half a troll! They'll get along plenty fine without her. This comes down to power and you know it!"

"Suppose I tell the trolls no," LaBelle said. "What happens then? Do you think the clan will accept that? She'll be hunted by the trolls and the Oak Hand. You think the Fold can hide her? Would you?"

"I absolutely would!" Dolly stomped her front hoof. "The trolls can have her when they pry her out of my cold, dead hands!"

"And they'd welcome the invitation," LaBelle shook his head. "Not just to kill you, but to come to the Above and destroy everything keeping them from Mira. And do you think that will go away just because we're in the right? And the Oak Hand will only gain more power if they don't have to hide the evils of Underfolk. It's hard enough for the Fold to survive without a civil war or an ongoing battle between us and the Oak Hand. If there was another way, I would jump on it…but no one is claiming rites of adoption."

"Because they're scared, LaBelle!" Irene said. "The trolls are claiming an ancient rite based on brutality! It'd be like if the Fae Queen only granted boons to those who could already do it themselves! And letting this happen because it's 'the law' is a pathetic excuse."

"If I don't do this, the Council will get involved and send her down anyway," LaBelle said with a wave of his hand. "It's inevitable."

"For someone who isn't afraid to die," Irene snapped, her wings buzzing, "you're a damn coward when things matter!"

The fairy flew off Dolly's shoulder and darted up through a vent over the griddle in the kitchen. LaBelle rubbed his face with his hand and took his hat off. Dolly folded her arms and stomped a hoof again, nearly cracking a floor tile.

"I hate this!" Dolly huffed. "She's just a kid, for the River's sake! If this were a fae child, then—"

"She's not a fae child!" LaBelle snapped, standing and pacing the restaurant. "I know we've all gotten attached to Mira, but she's still a member of the faction she was born to! We can't just pretend otherwise."

"Oh, that's so easy for you to say! You don't have a faction! They all look the same to you, but they're not! And I won't stand here and let Mira be taken by some thugs who assume they're all-powerful because of some archaic tradition that no one believes in anymore!"

"Would you risk your own life to give Mira that chance?" LaBelle asked, sourly. "A centaur and a troll would be a short fight. Do you love her enough that you would die for her?"

"I'm not saying I'd win," Dolly said, defeated, "but you could at least be angry about it!"

"Of course, I'm angry about it! You think I don't wish there was a way that everyone could get what they want? Mira doesn't deserve this, but I've been around long enough that—"

"Oh, spare me the 'holier than thou' wise man crap, for once! If you're not gonna do the right thing and I can't convince you otherwise, there's no point in you telling me that Mira deserves to be punished for existing. And she may last two years, but do you think the clan will let her leave? You're old, LaBelle, but you're so stupid, sometimes."

"Dolly, I'm sorry—"

"Don't apologize to me," Dolly shook her head. "Go apologize to Mira."

"I already—"

"No, you said you're sorry. That's different. If you won't fight for her, she deserves to think you feel bad about it. Go upstairs and talk to her right now," Dolly said, pointing at the staircase with a shaking finger. "Or…I'll never speak to you again!"

"Fine," LaBelle sighed, "but it won't change anything."

"Then you'll be no worse off than you already are," Dolly huffed, stomping one of her hooves. "You big brute."

LaBelle shook his head and walked up the stairs to the rooms. The ascent to the second floor of Dolly's diner was a struggle, as if his feet were made of concrete. He felt tired. He'd needed sleep before and he'd felt exhausted, but tired—with the world, with age, with his life —was a rare feeling that he was used to forcing down. This time, it was harder to ignore. He walked down the hall and paused in front of Mira's room. He listened for a moment and knocked on the door.

"Go away!" Mira snapped from inside.

"Mira, it's LaBelle."

"I said go away!" Mira repeated, firmer. "I'm not opening the door."

"Fine." LaBelle sat on the ground with his back to Mira's door. "Just listen to what I have to say. You know I could just walk in, so at least listen?"

"What do you want?"

"I'm sorry that we couldn't find a way to keep you up here. I know you're disappointed and scared, but—there's no other option, alright?"

"No, it's not alright!" Mira shouted through the door and LaBelle felt something heavy hit the wood, rattling the hinges.

"Mira, please," LaBelle said, "think about the people you met up here. You know how troll culture works. What would happen if you didn't come back?"

There was silence from the other side of the door for a minute. "The clan would come up."

"And they'd search every building," LaBelle continued, "every vehicle and every closet to find you. Before long, it wouldn't just be the Copper Tooth Clan anymore. There would be thousands of trolls running through the city with one goal and no authority to keep them in check. If we don't follow troll law, we're risking war. People like Dolly or Irene…even Matt and I would get caught in the crossfire."

"It's just not fair."

"I know," LaBelle admitted. " Look, I can try and make some assurances with the clan on behalf of the Council. It might take a while, but you'll be safe down there."

"It won't change them. Even if I know they won't kill me, I'll still be treated worse than garbage. Nothing changes."

"You'd have hope," LaBelle said. "When you're old enough, you can come up to the Above on your own. I just need you to wait until you're eighteen and there are more legal options. It's not the solution you want, but it's better to have hope than desperation."

LaBelle listened, still aware of Mira's quiet sniffling.

"What would your mother want?" LaBelle asked. "Would she want war or hope?"

Inside the room, floorboards creaked as footsteps moved close to the door. LaBelle stood up as the lock scraped open and he looked down at Mira. Her eyes were still red and puffy, wet with tears and her lower lip quivered. "I don't want anyone to die," Mira said. "I just don't want to go back to the troll caves."

"I know," LaBelle nodded, "but this is the way things are."

Mira rushed forward and wrapped her arms around LaBelle, startling him. He was expecting her to strike him or lash out. The possibility of a broken rib or two was an expected result of troll anger. Mira just wrapped her arms around LaBelle as she cried, her whole body shaking with tremendous sobs. LaBelle hesitated, but eventually put his hands on her back, hugging her. Matt was sitting on the bed when LaBelle looked up. The boy didn't look angry, but he wasn't pleased either. It looked like Matt was trying to solve some kind of puzzle or announce some brilliant idea to save the day, but he'd get nothing from LaBelle.

"It's not fair," Mira whined when she'd settled. "I just wanted a family. Is that too much to ask?"

LaBelle's heart softened. He'd lost count of the times he'd heard that question. "Is it too much to ask?" seemed to be a favorite complaint of mortals, as if the universe worked in checks and balances. Normally, LaBelle would say it was too much to ask and that low expectations were the secret to his happiness. Today, even he couldn't hide his disappointment.

"No," LaBelle said, rubbing Mira's back. "It's not."

Mira pulled away and wiped her face with the back of her hand. "I guess I should pack."

"We'll leave when you're ready," LaBelle said. "You can say goodbye to Dolly and Matt before we—"

"I'm coming with you," Matt said.

"Out of the question," LaBelle said, sternly. "You can wait here until I get Mira home."

"Mira just lost everything and she's going back to a hell you call home. I wouldn't be a good friend if I didn't stay with her through the hardest part."

"I want him to come," Mira urged. "If you're making me do this, can't you let him come?"

"And you're just going to wipe my memory, right?" Matt said. "What difference does another hour make if it means I can say goodbye to Mira properly?"

"This isn't a tourist experience," LaBelle said, calm as a frozen lake. "We're talking about one of the most dangerous parts of the Under."

"I don't care," Matt shook his head. "I'm going to be there for her and if you think Dolly will try and stop me, you underestimate her."

LaBelle sighed and nodded. "OK," he said, defeated. "You can come to say goodbye, but then it's all gone when you get to the Above again."

"And I want to remember Mira," Matt said, "for when she comes back."

"Fine," LaBelle said. "I'll do what I can."

"Thank you for trying," Mira told him, wiping her eyes again. "I guess I owe you that much. I'll try and pay you when I—"

"This one is on the house," LaBelle said. Even if Mira had property to call her own, LaBelle would have felt terrible for taking it. Making people pay for disappointment wasn't how he wanted to do business. "I'll give you two some time to pack everything up. I'll wait for you down in the diner and then we can take Matt's car to the Under Door at the Southend Spillway."

"Long drive," Matt said.

"I don't want to carry you through three levels of hell," LaBelle replied. "I'm doing you a favor by using the back door."

<u>Chapter 20</u>

"As soon as you turn eighteen," Dolly said, holding Mira's hands, "you come right up here and I'll have your room for you."

"May 12th," Mira nodded. "I'll mark my calendar."

Dolly hugged Mira tight. Mira squeezed back and Matt could see she was resisting the urge to cry again. This was the third time Dolly had said goodbye between Mira asking for the spare backpack, Dolly then insisting to help Mira pack her things, and the three of them going downstairs to an impassive LaBelle. When they finally finished hugging, Mira reached into her backpack and handed Dolly the big conch shell that sounded like the sea.

"No, keep it," Dolly said. "Something to look at and remember me."

"The clan wouldn't let me keep it," Mira frowned. "They'd probably break it. Besides, I don't need a shell to remember everything you've done for me."

"It'll be here when you get back." Dolly took the shell and forced a smile, wiping the tears away. Mira nodded and hugged Dolly a final time. She walked away with the backpack, unable to look the centaur in the eye. Turning from Mira and LaBelle, Dolly smiled at Matt. "And don't you be a stranger either."

"I'll be back before you know it," Matt smiled, though his heart wasn't in it.

"It was nice having both of you here while it lasted," Dolly said. She stepped forward and gave Matt a big hug as if he was an old relative. Dolly looked over at LaBelle. Her smile faded and her scowl made Matt uneasy. When she spoke, it was venomous. "Your tab is due at the end of the week. Don't be late."

"Understood," LaBelle said. His voice was quiet and calm, but Matt could see the clenched jaw and tight expression. LaBelle looked over to Mira and Matt. "Time to go."

Matt put a hand on Mira's shoulder and walked with her to the car out front. She almost got into the front seat, but LaBelle blocked her and slid in. As he drove, Matt half-listened to LaBelle's directions but spent most of the time looking at Mira in his rearview mirror. She looked sadly out the window, desperately trying to take in the details of the city around her. Her lips moved as she described everything, painting a mental picture that she could hold onto. The mirror turned away sharply and Matt looked over to see LaBelle tucking his wand back into his jacket.

"Eyes on the road, Matt."

The rest of the drive was silent. It took almost an hour to get to the furthest part of the city and Matt parked his car on the side of the Southend Spillway. When he was a freshman, Matt would come down here in the summer with his friends after heavy rain and throw rocks into the rushing water. The concrete channel was a popular spot for depositing old mattresses and busted tires, but Matt would never have thought it was a portal to a magical world. It smelled like low tide and garbage, the faint sounds of the city in the distance muffled by a long train whistle.

Matt staggered out of the car a little and watched LaBelle effortlessly slide down the concrete slope of the spillway. Mira hesitated, but eventually sat and slid down after him. Matt followed, but still felt a little banged up when he made it to the bottom.

"Last time I was here," Mira whispered to Matt, "I was running away from my clan. I didn't think I'd ever be here again."

"Nervous?" Matt asked her.

"Scared."

"Well, that makes two of us."

"Let's go," LaBelle grunted. "We're losing daylight."

"One more minute, please?" Mira asked. "I might not see the sky again for another two years. I'd like to remember it."

LaBelle let out a frustrated breath and folded his arms. "Alright, but we can't stay long."

Mira took off her mask and tilted her head back. Matt looked up with her. The sky was painted with reds and oranges, but tinged with purples stretching out like ribbons as the sun slowly set over the city. Matt never really watched the sunset anymore, but he knew Mira was preserving the memory. A seagull flew overhead, screeching out a final song of the Above.

"We should go," LaBelle said after a moment.

Matt looked over to Mira and she was crying again, big tears that dropped off her face and onto her shirt. LaBelle walked over and handed her a handkerchief. Mira wiped her eyes and took a few deep breaths before pocketing the scrap of cloth. With a nod, she followed behind LaBelle as they walked into the open mouth of the pipe that went down into the Under.

Together they stepped into the tunnel and the facade of the spillway faded like smoke dissipating in a strong wind. The ground was more natural than concrete and Matt realized that the dirt beneath his shoes was soft and moist. He could see campfires spread out in the distance. Turning to his left, Matt saw a massive shape curled up by the entrance that slowly uncoiled into a large, green reptile with a ring of horns around its head. LaBelle raised a hand to the dragon and the beast seemed to relax, but one of the bright, yellow eyes watched Matt.

"The dragons guard the furthest entrances," LaBelle explained, noting Matt's obvious fear. "They're more interested in keeping things from going out than coming in."

Other monsters appeared as they walked further into the Outerlands: a woman with leathery bat wings, a trio of green humanoids that only came up to Matt's waist, and a minotaur with long cow horns and armor made of car hubcaps. Most creatures avoided them, but the goblins had to be deterred with a stern look from LaBelle. Matt knew the purpose of their visit was an unpleasant one, but he still couldn't help but look around and take in the Outerlands of the Under. In the distance, Matt could make out small campfires and Mira's grip tightened around his hand as they approached.

"LaBelle!" a deep voice grumbled. Matt had to resist the urge to run as a giant creature approached them. The troll was seven feet tall and as broad as a bus. Parts of it were completely stone and the rest was covered in thick, leathery skin with fungal growths on the shoulders. Tufts of white hair dotted the troll's head and his eyes were the color of slate.

"I take more after my dad, I guess," Mira whispered as Matt looked over at her.

"Welcome home, halfbreed," the troll leader taunted Mira with a chuckle. "We were waiting for—"

"She's suffered enough, Dural," LaBelle snapped. "She doesn't need your words of cruelty."

Dural looked over to LaBelle and frowned. His attention turned to Matt and he snarled in disgust. "A human? In the Under? You go too far, LaBelle!"

"He's going to have his memory wiped, what's the difference?" LaBelle asked, exasperated. "Besides, he helped Mira against the Oak Hand. He's proven he can be trusted, if only with the bare minimum."

"Very well," Dural said, rolling his shoulders and sneering down at Matt. "Mira, say your goodbyes."

Mira was shaking and breathing quickly. Matt squeezed her hands and she turned to look at him, eyes wide and watery. He smiled weakly and hugged her tight. "Two years," Matt whispered in her ear. "Just hold on for two years and it'll be okay."

"I'll never forget what you did for me."

"I'll wait for you," Matt told her. He would have held Mira longer, but she was pulled away by the rough hand of the lead troll. Mira stumbled and fell, but didn't cry out or whimper. She rose from the ground with her backpack and walked over to an ancient troll woman standing in the clan. The older troll set a hand on Mira's shoulder and Mira bowed her head.

"And all is well," Dural affirmed with a deep rumble. "Now go."

"I want your word, Dural," LaBelle said like a cold wind, "that she'll be safe here. If I find out she's suffered any—"

"A bit of hard work is good for the soul," the troll leader said. The rest of the trolls laughed a little, but Mira shrank further into herself.

"Your word!" LaBelle roared, angrier than Matt had ever seen him. The shadows around him stretched longer and the fires struggled to fight the darkness that swelled around LaBelle's rage. LaBelle took a breath and spoke quieter, though the anger was still there. "I want your word she'll be safe."

Dural's smile faded and he scoffed. "You think me so cruel that I would harm one of my own?"

"I don't think that, but I know trolls too well. I'll be speaking with the Council. If word that she's harmed in any way gets back to me, I swear—"

"You'll what?" Dural asked. "She's not your concern anymore, LaBelle. Rest assured, she's no good to us dead."

"Dead is not what worries me," LaBelle said. Matt watched his fury soften and he looked at Mira with sadness. "I wish you nothing but the best."

Mira frowned and looked away, turning to the rest of her clan. LaBelle started leading Matt out of the tunnels with a jerk of his thumb and a guiding hand away from the trolls when he didn't instantly follow. Matt watched over his shoulder until Mira was nothing but a smudge of yellow raincoat in the darkness. Then she was gone.

They walked the rest of the way in silence. Matt no longer had the same interest or curiosity as they passed by the monsters that lived just under his home. Even the grandeur of the dragon guarding the entry had lost its luster. Without Mira, the world he was growing to love just felt flat. When they made it to the spillway, the sky was dark, streaked

222

with gray clouds that blended into the night sky. The lights of the downtown skyscrapers were flickering on like caged stars, but Matt only wished Mira could see it. The spillway was nothing but trash and emptiness.

"I know that wasn't easy," LaBelle finally spoke, "but it's better this way."

"Whatever helps you sleep at night," Matt said.

"Look, it wasn't just about the law, alright? Mira would never have been accepted by humans, you know that! She needed to be with the trolls."

"Do you hear yourself, LaBelle? She begged you to let her stay and you wouldn't even listen."

"It's not that simple!" LaBelle snapped. He paced a little and put his hands in his pockets. "Even if there was a way for her to stay, would humans ever accept her beyond a carnival act? Would she have been happy in a place so different from the world she grew up in?"

"You know she would have."

"You have a good heart, Matt," LaBelle sighed. "I hope you two find each other again."

"Just not when she lost everything and needs a friend the most?"

"Don't give me that. I didn't want to do this, but it's the way of the world! Even if the fairytales tell you that everyone gets what they want, sometimes it just doesn't happen. If the trolls would let her go? Maybe there's a way it would work, but I can't risk a civil war for one person! It's how it is…how it should be!"

LaBelle tightened his fist, grit his teeth, and kicked one of the nearby tires. He moved his hand through the air and conjured a fireball to throw at an abandoned mattress. After his outburst, he rubbed his face and sighed. The burning mattress glowed and Matt could see how frustrated LaBelle was in the flickering orange light. LaBelle dropped his hands and started walking back to the car. "It's been a long day. Let's just finish this."

"There's just one thing I don't understand."

"Only one? I guess that makes you quicker than most."

"If I asked you a question would you tell me the truth? If only because I earned that much?"

"I suppose that's fair," LaBelle said, walking further down the spillway. "Go ahead. I swear on everything I hold dear, you'll get the truth."

"Why didn't you tell Mira you were her father?"

LaBelle stopped walking and turned around slowly so the fire lit his face. To Matt's surprise, the man chuckled and shook his head. "You really are quick, you know that?"

Chapter 21

"So you admit it?"

"I promised you an honest answer," LaBelle nodded, holding out his hands as if to prove there weren't any tricks left. "How did you figure it out?"

"A few things," Matt said. "I started getting suspicious when the mermaid mentioned Mira's father wore a gray suit."

"Could have been a coincidence," LaBelle said, lifting the folds of his jacket. "It's a popular style. Besides, I showed you her father's grave."

"You said it yourself: lying comes easily to humans. I think that makes me better at spotting lies than Mira. And ever since the graveyard, you've been acting weirder and weirder. Every time she looks at you, you turn away. You're defensive, even protective of her.

You talk about loss and failure, but now it has a personal weight for you. Maybe you've known longer, but after you went down to the sphinxes? You've avoided the truth."

LaBelle sighed and walked over to Matt. He chuckled and looked up with a smile. "Seven thousand years and every so often I'm still impressed by humans."

"Why are you letting this happen, LaBelle? You could save her, you know she won't be happy there! What are you trying to hide? Are you too proud to admit that your daughter is half-troll?"

"It's not that easy," LaBelle sat on a stack of tires and folded his hands. "Mira's half-troll, but that's not why I can't claim her. I'm worried because she's also half-me."

"And what are you?"

LaBelle took a deep breath and sat up straighter. "I guess it doesn't matter what you know now. I'm old, Matt. Older than civilization, though I don't predate humanity. I come from a time when humans and Underfolk lived together, but not in harmony. There was a time before the schism that separated the Under and Above, a time before humans turned their enemies into nothing but stories. Before that, they needed the Guardians."

"Guardians?"

"What do you know about magic?"

"Not a lot," Matt confessed. "Magi use wands and stuff like that, but fae can pull it out of the air. Beasts don't care one way or another and humans don't know anything about it."

"Did you ever ask where it came from?" LaBelle pressed, eager. "No one ever thinks magic has a source anymore. The only ones who remember are a handful of ancient dragons and the Fae Queen herself. You see magic doesn't just exist. It's not mined from a mountain or from within a spell caster. Pure, untouched magic? That comes from humans."

"Humans?"

"Your emotions, to be specific. I think it was the Fae Queen who figured that out—or she was the one who started abusing that fact. The Fae Queen loves humans but views them more like batteries than living things. She would look at you and only see the emotional potential. That's why she loves children, all that raw emotion. No one feels joy, sadness, or anger in quite the same way as children do. The beasts could use magic back then, too, and did so often. They always thought fear was the strongest emotion and harvested it by hunting you for food."

"What about the magi?"

"They wouldn't come for another few hundred years after the Guardians," LaBelle shook his head. "See, the more the fae and the beasts harvested human emotion? The more powerful that magic became."

"Why couldn't humans stop giving them magic?"

"Have you tried rejecting an emotion? It's not as easy as flipping a switch."

"So, what did they do? If nothing happened, the Fae Queen would still be sucking the magic out of people."

"Well, it's not quite that. She thought she was doing you all a favor by giving humans eternal bliss. In reality, those of you who weren't under her spell were hunted by the beasts who wanted your fear. The more emotions, the stronger magic became. And so, magic created the Guardians."

"You talk about magic like it's alive."

"Yes and no," LaBelle shrugged. "Magic isn't just raw emotions, it's intention. You're happy *with* something, you're afraid *of* something. Humans took all that intention behind their emotions and formed something of an awareness. That awareness and pure magical energy created the Guardians…created me.

"I was born—I assume—in what we now call France. A group of nomads found me as a child and raised me as one of their own. We foraged and hunted what we could during the day, then slept fitfully at night, outrunning the monsters that lurked just beyond our fires. We were always afraid, always desperate, but we found moments of joy. Guardians were raised as humans so we could truly understand you. Not to act as some benevolent savior, but truly be of you. I knew I was an outsider, but they still loved me and I loved them. Until the giants came.

"There were three giants that descended on my clan while we slept." LaBelle rubbed his eye with the tip of his thumb and blinked. "I tried to run, but one caught me, threw me against the ground, and the

228

world went black. Some time passed and I woke on a pile of dead bodies. The giants were tearing my clan apart and eating them, piece by piece. You can't imagine the pain I felt then. I rose from that pile of bodies with a roar and the giants all stood to crush me again. On instinct, I reached out and felt magic pulsing through me. With a heave, I pulled lightning down from the sky and killed three giants with one strike.

"After I used magic, I felt others," LaBelle grinned. "I could sense them and see them wherever they were. They were my brothers and sisters. After the first death—the end of our human lives—we became something more and the magic within us woke up. Humans needed something to oppose the fae folk and the monsters. Magic gave birth to the Guardians. I was the only one of my kind in France, but I wasn't alone anymore.

"The reason I'm so respected, so feared," LaBelle continued, "is because I *am* magic. When a fae draws on magic or a magi casts a spell, they're using it as a tool. Magic is an extension of my form. Spells come as easy to me as blinking does for you. And that control over power? It scares people who want it.

"The dragons were the ones who called for peace," LaBelle explained, weaving his fingers together. "For a while, Guardians and humans were fighting a war on two fronts: the fae and the beasts separately. We fought, but we gave humans the gift of magic so they could fight with us. We made it possible to mix magic into human bloodlines and created the magi."

"The magi were human?" Matt asked.

"Once, yes, but we gave them the tools to use magic: wands, runes, and knowledge. With the magi and Guardians working together, the slaughter turned into a war. The dragons offered peace first, even threatening to join humans to defeat the Fae Queen if that was what it took. The Fae Queen was more responsive to that threat. We formed the first council and created the Under Pact: humans remain in the Above and the Underfolk would live underground where they could use magic. Humans would be able to thrive and the Underfolk still got their power. The monsters we used to call hunters were now safely away."

"And the magi?"

"They went down to organize the Under Cities," LaBelle said. "It started as a handful of magi in each Under City, but those in the Above came down and those in the Under thrived. Many beasts were resistant, but without the protection of their faction, they banished themselves to remote caves and the last few wilds of the world. The fae followed their queen and she went where the magic was. The Guardians remained above, teaching humans to defeat the monsters that once treated them as prey without having to create more magi."

"You taught humans how to kill Underfolk?"

"And they taught each other," LaBelle sighed, looking at the tree ring wrapped around his finger. "It wouldn't be until after the Crusades that we formed the Order of the Oak Hand."

"You're responsible for the Oak Hand?"

"We gave them knowledge as a tool—as a shield! But they turned it into a weapon. Needless to say, I was disillusioned with the moral strength of mankind after a few generations."

LaBelle looked down and wiped the inner corner of his eye with his thumb again. "Those that survived became the Underfolk. They banded together and built the Under Cities beneath human settlements to gather the magic. They formed a permanent Council and made their own laws. Mankind advanced in the Above, but magic was always drawn downward to those who would use it. Humans progressed, blissfully unaware of the power they gifted Underfolk in every breath they took."

"And what about the Guardians? Are they still around?"

"The last one is. See, the arrangement was going well for a while. The fae had their magic, the magi took what they needed, and the beasts surrendered magic before the Under Cities were created—only a handful of dragons still know how to use magic these days. For a while, we thought peace was possible until an oracle had a vision.

"Oracle visions are…" LaBelle searched for the right word, "Vague, but accurate. I don't much care for their work, but the Council takes an oracle's warning seriously. The Rain Prophecy completely upset the arrangement we'd had for centuries. According to one oracle, a Guardian would have a child. She didn't know which one of us and she didn't know when, but the child would topple the new order when they 'came of age.' It was described as the end of the Under. The

Council knew that any Guardian could parent this child. So, they hunted all Guardians."

"But Guardians are immortal, right?"

"Everything dies, Matt. Guardians are just humans with magic. When we had to use all our power against attacks from every faction of the Underfolk? Imagine a nuclear reactor going critical. The reactor doesn't survive either. We called it 'Ambustination'. I've seen the devastation that's left: craters the size of cities, whole chunks of cliff face torn from the side of continents. Hundreds of ambustination sites all over the world, but time has washed them away to nothing. And I felt each Guardian die with all the pain and fear that came with it."

"How did you survive?"

"I ran," LaBelle said. "When they were disorganized, the Underfolk were easier to fight. A random attack here and there was nothing to a Guardian, but when you're hunted by fairies, centaurs, trolls, dragons, vampires, elves, dwarves, and the rest of the Under? You can only fight for so long before you burst. There were huge losses—on both sides. It took a thousand of them to kill one of us, but they were willing to risk it for the new order. And there were so few of us already. It was only a matter of time before I was alone again.

"It was the Fae Queen who approached me," LaBelle sighed and rubbed his chin. "She was tired of all the fighting and wanted to make a deal. The magi thought that there was still a need for a Guardian. Back then, the Fold was wild and risky without any organization. The Under still had their fair share of squabbles between factions and they needed someone in the Above to uphold the Under Pact for humans. So, they said I could live. By agreeing, I became the mediator for all the problems between the Under and the Above. If there was magic or magical folk in the Above, I was called to settle their disputes. I was just, fair, and neutral.

"I survived," LaBelle said, his gaze distant and empty, "but I am the last of my kind. So, I did what we were meant to do. I helped Underfolk after I spent a hundred lifetimes forcing them below the surface. There's guilt there, so I try to stay out of modern affairs if it doesn't affect the Fold. I could have fixed the Above with a wave of my hand, but I didn't want to change the world with my immortality. I just needed to make it better one handful of people at a time."

"And the prophecy?" Matt asked. "Mira?"

"They said I could live as long as I bore no child. Even a half-troll, half-guardian has more power than the Fae Queen. And that is something the Under would fear. Do you understand now? If I acknowledge Mira as my daughter—bloodlines and all—it will put a bullseye on the back of her head for as long as she's alive."

"So, you did know her mother."

"Not as Kaysar," LaBelle smiled, nostalgic. "She was wearing a glamour when we met, but I could still see her. She only ever called herself Kate in the Above and I never pushed for her troll name. We met on one of her surface expeditions. She was up exploring the human world and I was there because I was bored and lonely."

"The Halloween party," Matt nodded. "The perfect hiding place for an Underfolk."

"And the place to meet other Underfolk," LaBelle smiled. "Meeting her was different. For millennia, I was this fearsome creature that lived under the bed or a whispered demigod that hunted Underfolk for sport and pleasure. I guess I hadn't been down to the Under for a long time, because she didn't care who I was. For a night, I was just Blanc. And she was simply Kate. We settled into our roles and played our parts a little too well. We fell for each other."

"That fast?"

"I'm old, not dead," LaBelle grinned. "We spent a year together on and off after the Halloween party. It was the only way I could keep her out of trouble, I think. It was strange, having this thing to look forward to after centuries of just existing. It was so different to have something to expect for once. And in that time, I fell more deeply in love with her than anyone else. And she fell just as hard. I was so used to being feared and she just—she understood me better than anyone had in a long time. She came up less and less until she stopped coming at all. I'm used to people leaving, so I didn't think twice of it. I never would have guessed Mira was the reason why."

"Seven thousand years and she was the only person you had a child with?"

"There was no one else like Kate."

"What made you fall in love with her?"

"It was how she appreciated the world. She was curious and got excited about the simple things I'd spent decades taking for granted. Not just the big things like phones and cars, but mundane things: clocks and tile floors. I mean, have you ever seen someone excited about a bottle of soda?"

"Yes," Matt nodded. "Mira."

"Matt—"

"I'm not saying you have to be Dad of the Year. I'm just asking you to help her. She needs you now, LaBelle. She came up here looking for her father—"

"If I take her as my daughter, the Council will kill her and me, just for good measure. If I tell her who I really am, she'll spend the rest of her life running."

"Then we'll figure something else out! Don't leave her behind to rot for two years in the hope that she won't be found. If this prophecy is true, with or without you there, she's going to end the Under. You want her to be safe? Save her now."

LaBelle shifted and took out his wand, casually holding it in both hands and considering it. "I could wipe your memory and make you forget this conversation ever happened. No loose ends."

"You could," Matt said, "but can you wipe your own memory? Cause if you want this to go away, then you have to get rid of any memory of Mira, too. And I don't think you want to do that because you know that Kaysar, your Kate, is gone and Mira is the only piece of her left. You can't afford to lose that, LaBelle. Mira is your last chance at happiness, at humanity. Maybe the pathway to peace needs you at peace, too."

LaBelle tapped his wand on his knee, frowning and glaring at a spot on the ground about three inches from Matt's feet. After a while, he stood, adjusted his coat, and turned back towards the Under Door.

"Come on, Matt," LaBelle said, cracking his neck. "Let's take one desperate chance."

Chapter 22

Matt stumbled to keep up, but LaBelle charged through the muck and dirt as if his feet weren't touching the ground. The detective marched through the Under Door and even the dragon shied away from his determination. The goblins ran from LaBelle and Matt, hiding behind anything they could to avoid the Guardian's fury. If it hadn't been for the pinpricks of light, Matt wouldn't have noticed when they came to the troll camp. By one of the fires, he could just make out Mira's yellow raincoat as the lead troll stood from his spot and approached the duo.

"LaBelle?" Dural grumbled. "Back so soon? I thought we—"

"Change of plans," LaBelle said, firmly. "She's coming with me."

"You have no—!"

"I swore I would get her to safety. With some reflection on the way out, I realized that 'safety' wasn't here with you or the clan. Mira may be half-troll, but the human half won't survive. I'm taking her back to the Above."

Mira was visible now, still clinging to her backpack and staying close to the older troll woman. Matt saw her wide eyes and fear was replaced by something else more inspiring. Matt could tell she was allowing herself to hope again. Dural was less thrilled.

"By what rite?" The troll leader growled.

"The Rite of She Should Be With People Who Care If She Lives Or Dies," LaBelle snapped. "It doesn't quite translate into troll, I'm afraid."

"We cannot allow this! You can't just take one of our clan!"

"Her bloodlines are severed," LaBelle proclaimed to the entire clan, "so her clan ties are contested. By your laws, she can be adopted by anyone she wants to leave with."

"By anyone who can survive trial by combat! And all troll combat is to the death! You, LaBelle, refuse to die."

"What can I say? It never took. But would you deny your clan the honor of fighting Blanc LaBelle in combat?"

"Victory without death is no victory," Dural snarled.

"How about this?" LaBelle exhaled, annoyed. "First to lose consciousness loses. I'm considered half-god in some cultures. If someone can beat me half to death? We'll call that a victory."

"Not if you're using magic!" Another troll yelled.

"I accept the terms," LaBelle stretched. "No magic: skill against skill. Let's get the initial rites out of the way. Mayza? If you would be so kind."

The older troll by Mira hobbled forward on her staff. Mayza raised her arms and proclaimed the challenge to the clan. "On this day, under the eyes of the Copper Tooth Clan, Blanc LaBelle has invoked the Rites of Adoption for Mira Copper Tooth. LaBelle? Do you accept the responsibility that comes with the Rites of Adoption?"

"I accept," LaBelle said.

"Mira," Mayza turned to the half-troll, "do you want LaBelle to adopt you?"

"Yes," Mira smiled, excitedly.

"Then the Rites of Adoption are affirmed! LaBelle, will you fight for yourself?"

"I always fight my own battles," LaBelle said, taking off his jacket.

"Dural, who will fight for the clan?"

"Roslah," a huge troll stepped forward, shaking his hand completely made of stone. "Let me fight him! I will knock the smug grin off his face!"

"If I'm fighting Kenos," LaBelle pointed at the eager troll, "I'd like a weapon. He's got a sledgehammer of a left hook."

"No magic," Dural shook his head, "but we will allow you a weapon to make it sporting."

"What a courtesy," LaBelle said, wrapping his hand around the end of his wand. With a quick pull, he drew the long blade from the palm of his hand. He spun the weapon in a flourish and tightened his fingers around the leather grip of his sword.

"By the ancient rite," Mayza declared, "this combat will decide the parentage of Mira Copper Tooth. Prepare yourselves!"

LaBelle handed his coat, wand holster, and hat to Matt, then drove the point of his sword into the ground to roll up his sleeves. "Stay by Mira," LaBelle whispered to Matt, "just in case."

"In case what? You won't die, right?"

"I'm more concerned about your safety," LaBelle said. "Trolls aren't renowned for their sense of fair play. You are a liability while I can't protect you. I'd rather have you close to Mira and Mayza. They'll ensure you aren't hurt while I can't watch out for you."

LaBelle took his sword out of the ground and gave it a few experimental swings. Matt watched the towering troll, Kenos, slam his fist into the ground and snarl at his opponent. As the trolls crowded the fight, Matt walked carefully around the inside of the circle so he could keep close to LaBelle. Most of the trolls growled and one tried to block Matt's path with a road sign ax. Urgently, Matt side-stepped the heavy blade and rushed over to Mira and the older troll. Mayza blocked Matt and bared her tusks with a glare. Matt took a step back, but Mira put a hand on the troll woman's arm. "Matt's my friend."

Mayza relaxed and took a step back. Matt moved past her and hugged Mira. She squeezed tightly and pressed her face into his shoulder. "I never thought I'd see you again."

"I wasn't gonna let that happen," Matt assured her.

"What is he thinking?" Mira asked, turning back to the fight. "Why did LaBelle change his mind?"

Matt looked between Mira and LaBelle for a minute before shrugging. "Who knows what goes on in LaBelle's head? The guy just challenged a troll to as close as he can get to a death match."

"And if it were anyone else? I'd be more worried. You should go too, just in case."

"No," Matt shook his head. "I have faith in LaBelle and I'm not leaving you here."

###

LaBelle walked up to Kenos, the largest troll of the clan with a white mohawk. Kenos slammed his stone fist against the ground and roared. LaBelle swung the sword, trying to decide on the exact style to use. If he was dealing with another swordsman, he'd favor French fencing, but the brutality of troll fighting required strength rather than precision. Trolls were big and clumsy, but even one strike would be enough to knock him off balance. LaBelle raised the blade, saluted Kenos and then Mayza. The tuckra nodded and raised her staff. LaBelle took one more breath and focused on Kenos when he heard the final command from Mayza. "Begin!"

Sprinting forward, LaBelle wanted to use one good burst of speed before the troll's strength could overwhelm him. Kenos swung his stone fist and LaBelle ducked, cutting his blade deep into the troll's exposed left side. Dark purple blood seeped out from the cut and spilled onto the dirt floor, but the wound healed over with a layer of stone instantly, stopping the bleeding. Kenos swung his stone fist and LaBelle parried the blow, sending tremors up his arm. LaBelle jumped to the side and rolled, avoiding another strike from the rocky appendage. Hopping to his feet, LaBelle spun the sword and switched to a defensive stance.

Kenos roared and charged again, swinging his giant fist. LaBelle sidestepped right into the troll's open hand and felt the massive fingers crush his torso. Kenos threw LaBelle's body hard against the ground, kicking up dirt when he made impact. His ribs were probably broken, but it only took a moment to block out the pain. LaBelle heard the words of an old fighting instructor in his mind. "Work through the pain. Survive, then hurt."

LaBelle shook his head to bring the world back into focus. He rolled onto his back in time to see Kenos's massive fist about to come down on his stomach. LaBelle somersaulted backward before the stone hand slammed into the dirt. LaBelle swung his sword at Kenos's face, forcing the troll away long enough for him to stand. Kenos threw a feral left hook and LaBelle held his defensive position. Kenos's attacks were violent and wild, throwing punches and trying to grab LaBelle when he proved to be too fast.

His experiences with the Vikings had taught LaBelle that blocking was harder than deflecting, so he used the flat edge of his sword to lessen the strength of Kenos's blows. He relied on old Shadow Walking techniques that the vampires had taught him to avoid conflict and sidestep attacks. The troll's robust scent was easy to track and LaBelle followed his opponent's position as the werewolves had taught him. Years of studying were reduced down to what he could remember about troll anatomy to try and find a weakness.

LaBelle's mind was too distracted and he felt a hard blow on the side of his face. The impact knocked him off his feet and LaBelle's head was ringing as he groaned in the dirt. LaBelle blinked a few times and shook his head to clear his vision. Kenos was raising his hands with a yell and other trolls cheered him on. Only Mira was looking at him and his vision cleared again.

No, LaBelle told himself. *This isn't the end.*

Climbing to his feet, LaBelle felt a sharp pain in his jaw and could tell his eye was already swelling. He lifted his sword again, raising the blade and pointing the tip at his opponent. When the troll turned back, Kenos slammed his stone fist into the ground. LaBelle thought about what he'd seen of the troll so far. Kenos favored his left swing, leaning back before throwing a punch to add strength. Striking the stone hand opened the troll up to attack, but LaBelle would exhaust himself before the blade would hurt Kenos. If the brute couldn't bleed, there were other ways.

LaBelle forced Kenos to advance with a yell. The troll raised his massive hand to crush him, but LaBelle ducked under the blow and kept running. LaBelle swung his sword and slashed Kenos's left Achille's tendon. The wound hardened over into stone, but the tendon was still severed within.

Kenos roared and fell to one knee. As the troll splayed out his right hand to support his weight, LaBelle drove the point of his sword into Kenos's flesh, pinning the troll's arm in place. Kenos swung his stone arm around and LaBelle jumped onto the troll's shoulders to avoid the blow. Pound for pound, LaBelle knew he'd never be able to fight a troll with brute strength. He had to be smarter.

LaBelle tightened his legs around Kenos's neck and growled. The troll's stone hand reached up to grab him, but LaBelle took hold of the stiff, clumsy fingers. In Greece, LaBelle had wrestled champions and heroes, but their strength was nothing compared to wrestling with the troll. LaBelle focused most of his strength on his legs, keeping them tight around the troll's neck to cut off the airflow. The stone hand fought him, but LaBelle only spared enough to keep Kenos at bay.

Kenos thrashed his head, trying to throw LaBelle off as the Guardian held firm. Kenos's breathing was getting rougher as the troll tried to fight and LaBelle could feel the strength in the stone hand waning. Kenos fell onto his back and LaBelle swung around to kneel on Keno's windpipe. LaBelle crushed the troll's throat with his knee and looked up at Dural.

"Call the fight!" LaBelle yelled. "It's over, Dural! Don't make me kill him!"

Dural scowled but finally nodded. Mayza stamped her staff against the ground twice and most of the trolls groaned, but LaBelle heard a few who were satisfied with the display. He climbed off Kenos's chest and limped over to the assembly of trolls with a scowl. The trolls that were upset quieted and backed away from LaBelle as he approached the clan leader. The only sounds were the crackling fire and Kenos's ragged wheezing on the ground to catch his breath. LaBelle drew his sword from Kenos's hand, leaving a splash of blood on the ground as the blade faded away from the rest of the wand.

"Now," LaBelle said, looking at the roslah, but speaking to the clan, "will you honor our agreement?"

Dural rumbled deeply and LaBelle felt the distaste vibrating through the air. "Very well," the roslah finally snarled. "She is yours. The adoption is accepted."

"Glad we could come to a civilized agreement," LaBelle said, spitting some blood on the ground. He limped towards Mira and Matt, took his hat from the young boy, and set it on his head. He turned and forced a smile for the clan tuckra. "Mayza, it was a pleasure. I hope my next visit is less exciting."

"Likewise, LaBelle," Mayza said. "Treat her kindly. If you don't? I'll know. And then you'll wish Kenos could have killed you."

"I don't doubt it," LaBelle winced. "Let's go, Mira."

Mira picked up her backpack and looked at the troll tuckra. The older troll smiled and wiped a stray tear off Mira's cheek with a careful finger. "Be brave, little one," Mayza said. "Your mother would be so proud of you."

"Thank you," Mira said, smiling. She rushed over and urged Matt to follow her towards LaBelle. None of the trolls stopped them, but a few started to disperse now that the fight had ended. Once the teens were at his side, LaBelle turned and led everyone out of the troll camp. The trolls parted to let them go by, a few rushing past them to help the wounded Kenos. LaBelle limped most of the way, feeling parts of his body already bruising.

"LaBelle—" Mira began.

"Not yet," LaBelle grimaced. "It's taking a lot of concentration to not pass out right now."

"I just…thank you."

"Well, another three paces and you can pay me back."

"How?" Mira asked.

"Don't let me fall," LaBelle said, stumbling in the dark. Mira caught LaBelle's weight on her shoulder while Matt took the other side and LaBelle smiled at him, a shared understanding finally reached. "Thank you."

"Let's get you to a hospital," Matt suggested.

"I just need a good night's sleep," LaBelle said, "and some time to lick my wounds. Get me back to my apartment, I have everything I need there."

"Can we make one pit stop first?" Mira said. "I have a promise to keep."

Chapter 23

LaBelle pressed the raw steak against his face and grimaced. After the pain flared in his eye, he relaxed and let out a deep breath.

"That should help with the swelling," Dolly said, wiping her hands on a towel. "At least until you get a chance to clean yourself up."

"Thanks, I'll pay you for the steak."

"Don't worry about it," Dolly smiled. "I'll put it on your tab."

LaBelle grinned and let out a breath. Mira and Matt were sitting at the counter, talking excitedly. Dolly had broken into what was left of the bakery case, presenting everyone with an array of celebratory donuts, cupcakes, and muffins. Matt and Mira were taking turns telling Daryl and Irene the story again while LaBelle nursed the surface wounds he could tend to at the diner.

"It's so good to have you back," Dolly smiled, squeezing Mira in a tight hug. "I could feel something happening, but couldn't tell what! I was pacing a hole in the floor waiting for someone to come and tell me what was going on."

"I'm just glad to be back," Mira said. "Mayza was nice, but I can only stand so much of that tea. I should go unpack! I want to get back to working at the restaurant tomorrow. If I'm gonna live up here, I gotta pull my weight."

"Actually," LaBelle cleared his throat and lowered the steak off his eye. "I'm wondering if you wanted to come live with me?"

"With you?" Mira asked.

"I got a spare room," LaBelle shrugged. "Since I adopted you by troll law, I'm responsible for your well-being. It'd be easier to keep an eye on you if you were close by. And if you lived there, Dolly could pay you with money rather than room and board. If, of course, you don't mind having a grumpy old man as a roommate."

"Dolly?" Mira asked. "What do you think?"

"I think that's a great idea, but you should run up to your old room and grab that shell off your nightstand. I left it there for you."

Mira grabbed Matt's arm and the pair rushed up the stairs with Irene fluttering close behind them. Daryl wiped his beard clean of crumbs and waddled back to the kitchen, collecting the last of the plates used in the celebration. LaBelle chuckled and pressed the steak back against his eye. When he opened his other eye, Dolly glanced down at him with a broad smile. "What are you so smug about?"

"I knew you'd do the right thing," Dolly grinned. "I didn't have a feeling, I just felt like you would. Even if I wasn't sure when."

"Well, I won't lie and say you didn't encourage me to make the right choice," LaBelle pulled the meat away, "but if I'd listened to you sooner, I might not have the black eye."

"We'll say that's a lesson you needed to learn. And if all you pay for it is a black eye and a steak, I think that's a cheap price."

"Next time, I'll go to Dolly's School of Bright Ideas before the Troll School of Hard Knocks."

"Be glad you made it out this time," Dolly folded her arms and looked up towards the staircase. "You took a real risk for her."

"It's not like I would have died."

"No, but this was a bold move for you. Underfolk won't believe you're completely impartial anymore."

"No, I guess not," LaBelle sighed, "but I've been on the sidelines for too long. It's about time I took a side on something. The beauty of not being affiliated with a faction is that I don't have to follow their laws when I feel they're wrong. We can help more people now that I advertised that fact."

"That's a relief," Irene said, coming down and standing on the countertop. "Things at the office were a little slow and this should bring in some much-needed business!"

"You think so?" LaBelle laughed. "I was ready to post ads for a new secretary."

"As if you could find someone else to suffer your shenanigans," Irene laughed. "But it'll be nice seeing people at the office! I feel like this is a fresh start for us!"

LaBelle smirked and looked back to the staircase, checking for Matt and Mira. "Dolly? Irene? There's something I need to tell you both."

"I know it's not perfect," LaBelle said, leading the teens into his apartment, "but I think it's better than troll caves. Once I've had a chance to recover, I can turn the study into a real room for you."

"This is great!" Mira beamed, setting her backpack down on the living room couch. Matt followed behind her and looked around the apartment. He saw ancient Greek swords, stacks of Spanish doubloons, and other museum-grade curiosities interspersed between common books that Matt had seen on his parent's bookshelf. Irene fluttered out of LaBelle's coat pocket and into a glass terrarium with a hand-built house of juice boxes and soda cans. The fairy seemed quite at home in the container.

"And the diner is just a short walk away," LaBelle noted. "I can drop you off every morning on my way to the office."

"Thanks, LaBelle," Mira said. She looked around, overwhelmed with excitement and trying to contain giddy laughter. "I can't believe I have a home now!"

"Irene?" LaBelle said, walking into the kitchen. "Why don't you help Mira get settled in? I have to talk with Matt quick. Check that old steam trunk in my room for pillows and blankets."

"Come on, Mira," Irene flew in quick circles around the half-troll, "if you like reading, you're gonna love the study!"

Mira smiled and grabbed her backpack, chasing after Irene as the fairy rushed down the hall. Matt turned back as LaBelle pulled out a bottle from a cabinet and poured some thick green fluid on a pale rag. The detective pressed the cloth against his head and sighed. LaBelle opened his other eye and grinned.

"So," Matt swallowed. "What now?"

"Now? You should get back home," LaBelle said, pressing the cloth to his eye. "Your parents must be wondering where you've been all day."

"No memory wipe?"

"No memory wipe. I trust you to do the right thing. However, I ask one favor."

"Name it."

"Don't tell Mira," LaBelle said. "I'm not ready for that conversation yet. I might be in the future, but not now. Her safety is more important than that knowledge. I need your word. I trust you, but you have to swear that you won't tell her."

"I won't tell her, I swear," Matt shook his head. "Does anyone else know?"

"Dolly knows," LaBelle said. "Irene knows, too, but no one else and I'd like to keep it that way. I'd rather keep this between the people who deal with her often enough that they might notice. And I won't have to look too far if word gets out."

"I don't want to lie to Mira," Matt said. "She's my friend, too."

"Take a lesson from the fae," LaBelle said, pulling his cloth away to reveal a much less swollen eye. "No lies, only half-truths if you have to avoid lies and don't let people ask too many questions. Do we understand each other?"

"I think we're perfectly clear."

LaBelle nodded and took a sip of the green, healing liquid. He grimaced at the taste and looked back at Matt when the flavor passed. "You should get home. I'm sure I'll see you around."

"Just one more question?" Matt started. "Can we do anything about that seed pod?"

"The what?"

"That bean thing you had me swallow on the first day? The one that keeps me from telling people about the Underfolk?"

"Oh, that!" LaBelle smiled. "I made that up."

"You made it up?"

"I don't often meet people who know nothing about magic," LaBelle chuckled. "You can't blame me for having a little fun."

###

Matt was exhausted when he made it back home. The full weight of the day hit him as soon as he shut off his car. The cemetery, the troll caves, and Mira's homecoming had all happened in the time it took for Matt to break his eleven o'clock curfew. His mom had called twice without leaving a message. She only did that when she was really mad and wanted Matt to know it. Unlocking the door to his parents' unit, Matt prepared for the worst. His mother shot upright from the kitchen table and blocked him from going any further. "Matt! Where have you been? I've been worried sick!"

"I quit the grocery store," Matt said. "I knew you'd be upset about that, so I needed to clear my head for a bit and figure some things out."

"You quit? Why?"

"I couldn't deal with it anymore. I hated working through all this. They pay us crap and the people we have to serve are even worse. I had to get out of there, Mom. It wasn't where I wanted to be."

His mom frowned and walked over to him. Matt braced for more yelling and anger, but she gently put her arms around him.

"I wish you told me," she said. "I mean, you didn't sign up for this crisis. You took the job to stock groceries for pocket money, not supply for a disaster. At worst, you were supposed to handle an old lady who was angry over coupons. I don't blame you for wanting to quit. Your dad and I wanted you to take this job so you could learn to be responsible. And part of being responsible is knowing when you need to take care of yourself. If you don't want to work there anymore, you don't have to."

"Really?"

"Of course not, Matt. You should have just talked to me about it."

"I'm sorry I kept it from you," Matt said. "I'm looking for another job, but—"

"Most of your life has been turned upside-down this year," Mrs. Brand said. "You deserve a rest and time to focus on school now that classes are starting in the fall."

"I might still go out," Matt said. "Drive around so I don't feel trapped."

"I don't see why not," Mrs. Brand said, "but tell me these kinds of things in the future. And you still have to stay safe and healthy: six feet, masks and all that."

"I promise, I won't be anywhere near someone who has the possibility of the virus," Matt agreed. "Thanks for understanding."

"Oh, good news!" Mrs. Brand said. "Your dad got a negative test! He's got a flight back tomorrow morning. He's gonna have to stay in quarantine at Uncle Will's for a bit, just to be safe, but he'll be back before you know it!"

"That'll be great," Matt smiled. "It's been a long day, so I think I'm gonna call it a night."

"Goodnight…and hey! No more lying, got it?"

"No more lying," Matt nodded, remembering LaBelle's advice. He brought his bag to his room and dropped it onto his bed. He would have to return his apron in the morning, but he wasn't too bent up about leaving the grocery store. It was a dead-end job that he'd leave in a few years and now he'd be able to explore the world that meant a lot more than which soup cans were on sale. His phone vibrated and Matt picked up the call from Mira.

"Hey," Matt answered. "How is it at LaBelle's?"

"I thought living at Dolly's place was good!" Mira said and Matt could hear the joy in her voice. "LaBelle has so many books! And Irene is gonna help me get new clothes, Dolly is gonna start paying me…tonight turned out so much better than this afternoon made me think!"

"I'm glad you're happy. After all this, you deserved some good news."

"Anything is better than the troll caves," Mira said. "Sorry about your job though."

"Eh, it wasn't the end of the world. The good news is I have more time to hang out with my new best friend while we figure her new life out."

"Sounds like a plan. How about tomorrow?"

"As long as we avoid getting kidnapped? Sounds like fun."

Chapter 24

Mira hung up her phone and put it on the desk by her backpack. LaBelle's study was warm with wooden bookshelves, a dark leather couch, and a big oak desk with brass knobs. Mira's room at Dolly's was simple and comfortable, but something about this study felt more welcoming. It felt like a place she could call home. She walked over to one of the shelves and ran her finger along the spines. After considering for a while, she picked one off the shelf and wrapped herself up in a blanket to read on the couch. LaBelle knocked on the door cautiously and walked in when Mira murmured her permission.

"Not tired?" LaBelle asked, smiling. Compared to an hour ago when he was in the troll caves, he looked a lot less like he was about to die.

"Afraid not," Mira said. "I'm kind of a night owl."

"Well, at least we won't have to worry about keeping each other awake. I just need to grab something from the desk, if you don't mind?" LaBelle walked over to the desk and opened a drawer, taking out a small, leather parcel. He put the pouch in his pocket and pointed to the book in Mira's hands.

"I liked that one," LaBelle said. "Dickens was one of my favorites. I think he would have liked you."

"Sorry, I should have asked, but—"

"It's fine. I'm glad you feel at home. I have this bad habit of hoarding things like books. No one is ever around to enjoy them. A lot of these antiques have stories I've never gotten to tell. Maybe having you here will give me a reason to talk about them more."

"Have you met anyone else famous?" Mira asked.

"I've been a background figure for a lot of the unforgettable moments of history," LaBelle sat on the edge of the desk and rested his foot on the chair. "Da Vinci, Alexander the Great, Einstein, even Blackbeard."

"Really? Blackbeard?"

"That was back when I was pirating off the coast of the new American Colonies," LaBelle smiled. "I met Blackbeard when I transitioned from attacking Spanish gold ships to taking slave trading vessels."

"Why did you make the switch?"

"I had fewer problems killing slave traders than gold shufflers," LaBelle grinned. A bell rang from the living room and he grumbled. "A story for another time, I fear. Duty calls."

"Everything alright?"

"Nothing to worry about," LaBelle assured her, grimacing a little as he stood. "The job never sleeps, I'm afraid."

"Is it about me?"

"I'm not sure," LaBelle admitted. "The Council probably just wants to have a stern word with me about challenging a troll to combat. That sort of news travels fast. Don't worry, I've survived worse scoldings before. Think about anything you want for your room and we'll see about getting it tomorrow morning."

"Thanks, LaBelle," Mira said, resting on the couch again.

"Ya know, you could call me Blanc, if you like."

"Hmmm," Mira thought. "I kinda like LaBelle better. Maybe I'll save Blanc for when you're in trouble"

LaBelle laughed. "Deal. I'd appreciate knowing if you're mad at me before starting a conversation. I'm still getting used to a roommate apart from Irene."

"Sounds like a deal," Mira said. "Goodnight, LaBelle."

"Night, Mira," LaBelle smiled and closed the door behind him. Mira settled into the couch and cracked open the book again, listening to the sounds of the ocean coming from the conch shell on the desk.

"I understand that the Council is upset!" LaBelle said, pacing the ethereal chamber. "I still feel what I did was in everyone's best interest."

"The trolls are furious!" Extoran snarled, slamming his claw into the ground and leaving massive cracks under his foot. The dragon hissed and spread his wings menacingly.

"Settle, Extoran," the Fae Queen sighed, unimpressed. "Your anger is smothering me."

"Of course, the child thief is content to leave this act unpunished!"

"Enough!" Aili yelled. "The Council Realm is not a battlefield. We cannot resort to violence here or declare an act of violence within this place."

"LaBelle swore he would bring Mira back to the trolls!" Extoran growled.

"No," LaBelle corrected the dragon bluntly. "I said I would ensure her safety. Upon examination of the situation, after I brought her back to the trolls, I decided she was safer on the surface with the Fold."

"We should have been consulted!" The blue dragon roared, punctuating his anger with a deep growl. "The Outerlands fall under our jurisdiction! Dural feels cheated and says you dishonored his clan!"

"I respected their rules," LaBelle said. "It's one half-troll child. If the clan struggles to recover from her absence, then they aren't as strong as they claim. And I'll stand by my choices. Mira is staying with me. End of discussion."

"Why you, insolent—!"

"I agree with LaBelle," Aili said, cutting through the dragon's rage with a calm voice. "Mira is safest on the surface with him. He made the promise that he would protect her. Where is safer than under the care of a guardian?"

"You would let him keep Mira?" Extoran asked, surprised.

"If he adopted her according to troll tradition, I'll say he earned that much," Aili said. "We told LaBelle that our interest was the safety of all our denizens. We need to remain aware that sometimes tradition does not mean right. Mira wants to stay with LaBelle—Mayza confirms that. I say we allow the adoption. Mira is an unusual case and this requires unusual solutions."

"I agree," the Fae Queen said. "LaBelle had Mira's best interest at heart when he offered to adopt her. It's worth trying, at least."

"There's still the matter of Matt," Extoran growled, realizing he'd been beaten. "Raska the Green has told me that LaBelle brought the boy into the Under. LaBelle endangers us all with—"

"Matt isn't a threat," LaBelle assured. "In fact, I think it will be better to have him around."

"You swore!" Extoran snarled, the growl rumbling in his throat. "Only Mira's father would learn of our existence and you would clean up any messes you made. That boy is a mess that needs cleaning!"

"If I recall correctly," LaBelle turned to the dais of the Magi Prima, "I said 'only one human would have to learn about our world,' did I not?"

The wizard with the white beard flipped through his large book on their podium, his brow furrowed and his eyes tense. After a moment of scanning pages, the wizard set a finger on a line and moved his lips as he read the previous meeting's record to himself.

"LaBelle is correct," the ancient wizard nodded. "There is no breach of his word."

"Is it wise to include Matt, if he's not necessary?" The Fae Queen asked. "The Council knows very little about him beyond second-hand accounts from a handful of Underfolk."

"I will vouch for him personally," LaBelle said.

"Do you?" The Fae Queen smiled. "Interesting. Why?"

"I like to think—after all my time with humans—I've become a good judge of character. I made Matt promise to keep the Under secret and I trust him to keep his word. He's a good friend for Mira and she'll need a guide to the human world."

"And you're not that guide?" Aili asked, allowing a tiny smile.

"A guide to the Above? Perhaps. But a guide to modern teenagers? I wouldn't begin to suppose I'm qualified. She'll be happier if she can start this transition with a friend."

"Agreed," Aili nodded. "It's a calculated risk, but I trust LaBelle to tie up any loose ends."

"Some of LaBelle's favorites in the past have turned against us all," the Fae Queen said with a rare frown. "However, the boy deserves the chance to prove himself."

LaBelle turned to the dragons for their decision. Extoran snarled and folded his wings. "This will not be the last time LaBelle's interference brings us trouble. A dangerous precedent has been set. Already the beasts are surging towards the surface. We can maintain that barrier between the Under and the Above for now, but we will not be held responsible for whatever comes of this."

"Then for now," Aili said, "the Council agrees. LaBelle will be responsible for Mira's safety, health, and well-being. We will revisit this at a later date, if necessary. LaBelle, we'll be watching you. This isn't a free pass. This is a warning."

"I understand," LaBelle said, bowing his head.

"Then let us retire," the Fae Queen stretched. "I grow weary of this."

The Council slowly disappeared, leaving only Extoran, Aili, and LaBelle. The Great Dragon towered over LaBelle, but only snarled at the guardian. "You were lucky this time, but if anything goes wrong? It will be blood on your hands."

"If saving Mira's life comes at a cost? I'll pay it."

Extoran snorted again and took off from the dragons' platform. Before disappearing, LaBelle heard a final resonating roar that he felt in his chest, triggering a flicker of ancient fear. When the roar faded, he turned back to Aili and smiled. "Thank you."

Aili sighed and looked to the storm that Extoran had vanished into. "They're right, you know. The only thing keeping the beasts from going to the Above was tradition. Letting Mira up there is a dangerous exception that may encourage more to try and leave the Under."

"As I said," LaBelle mused, walking with Aili in the realm, "I'll accept it."

"LaBelle, what is she to you? In all the time I've known you, you've never been willing to take a risk like this. You've had your handful of allies and apprentices, but no one completely in your care as a ward. Something about this girl is different. What is it?"

LaBelle sighed and rubbed his chin. "She reminded me of someone. And she asked for help."

"Others have asked you for help."

"Not in a way that made me think," LaBelle said. "I have to keep as many people safe as I can. I lost sight of that somewhere along the way. I was meant to be an agent for all factions, but instead, I went numb to everything and did nothing."

"You helped the Council."

"The Council doesn't need my help. They never did. I need to take care of people like Mira: the displaced and alone. I'm not changing our arrangement, Aili, but I want to focus my efforts. I can do good up in the Above and it would bring me back out of the dark."

Aili nodded and took a deep breath. "I'm glad this girl affected you, LaBelle. I just hope it doesn't get you killed."

"If it does, it would be a surprise to us both."

"What shocks me is you introducing a new factor into your life. I thought you were one to keep things the same and now you're adopting a teenager. If you thought that would be easy, you can kiss your routine goodbye."

LaBelle laughed and the sound echoed through the Council Realm. "Well, I'm old enough to know that the only constant is change. Maybe you'll learn that when you're a bit older."

Acknowledgements

I would like to thank a number of people for their help with this project.

Forest, Devon and Libby: Thank you all so much for reading this story and getting it polished enough for the rest of the world. This is truly a labor of love and I was so excited not only to have a final product, but to be able to share it with you. I'm so appreciative of you jumping into the Under with me.

Thanks to Emily Congdon for the fantastic cover design! It's absolutely stunning and I love how it turned it. You went above and beyond and I can't thank you enough for the effort you put into this project. Find more of Emily's work at <u>emilycongdon.com</u>

Author Biography

Nicholas Westbrook is a writer living in Connecticut. He is a graduate of Roger Williams University and Southern Connecticut State University with degrees in Creative Writing and Library Science, respectively. He enjoys playing Dungeons & Dragons, should not be left alone in bookstores, and will usually greet dogs before their owners. More of his writing can be found at www.nwwestbrook-writing.us, where you will also find links to all his social media.